Spring Ir

CW00391987

2020 Eunuon

With Stories from:

Ian Hugh McAllister

David Rogers

Vincent Morgan

Owen Morgan

Margaret Karmazin

Gary Wosk

Bob Ritchie

Erin Lale

James Pyles

Alex Minns

Charles Venable

Elizabeth Houseman

Tony Conaway

Special Foreword from Sandy Stuckless

Cover Design by:

Steger Productions

https://fantasyandcoffee.com/SPDesign/

Published by:

Cloaked Press, LLC

PO Box 341

Suring, WI 54174

https://www.cloakedpress.com

All rights reserved.

ISBN: (Paperback) : 978-0-9991690-9-4

CONTENTS

FOREWORD
BY SANDY STUCKLESS

Hello all! Hope you are well. I'm going to keep this short and sweet because the words you're about to read from the magnificent authors in this anthology are far more interesting than anything I can tell you.

Science fiction for me comes down to one simple thing: Exploration. Exploration of things that don't exist yet, of things that may never exist. Exploration of the human mind. You can go from deep space in one instance, to the dark web in the next. You can explore aliens, humans, or robots in a multitude of scenarios that keeps the imagination humming. The endless possibilities are a beautiful thing. And despite all of those possibilities, you always end up back at the same place. Human connection. With Spring into Scifi 2020, you're going to find that beauty and that connection! Enjoy!

–Sandy R. Stuckless-
Appeared in:
Spring Into SciFi 2018 "Date Night"
Fall Into Fantasy 2019 "Unfollowed"
Twitter: @SandyRStuckless
Facebook: https://www.facebook.com/SandyRStuckless

FRINGE BENEFITS
BY IAN HUGH MCALLISTER

TravelSpace ended abruptly, accompanied by the usual gut-wrench. I fought back the usual brief wave of nausea, reaching the point where I tasted lunch again before choking it back. I hate TravelSpace, but it gets you to where you need to be without HiberSleep, which jumps your timeline.

The local port authority were on to us in seconds. Maybe we should have repainted the spacecraft dark grey, but Amisool insisted that a Sendian Light Clipper in chartreuse was the only way to be seen, even after we stole the thing in the first place. Well, to be fair I didn't steal it, he did. I was part of the previous crew, off-duty and sleeping while the owner and the rest of them partied it up at Fry's Bar on Dantel-Mitschoff. You know, the planet with the pink rings. I woke up to find I'd been press-ganged because Amisool had helped himself to the ship. I guess that makes him either a pirate or hijacker and because I stayed on as his sole crew member, it probably made me indictable as his accomplice. If we ever get apprehended, I'm definitely claiming to be his hostage.

Where was I? Oh, yes, I was telling you we'd stand out and be seen in the green. Yeah, well I was right on that one. Amisool was waving three arms around; just the three, because the other one gripped a very large cocktail. One huge hand hammered the drive console. "Oh, for the love of sentience! Where did they spring from? Oh well, sweat the small stuff, Ranns," he offered. "We'll walk away with a ticket for not filing a transit request in triplicate, or whatever else passes for bureaucracy in this particular armpit of the galaxy. What's the worst that can happen?"

"Come on, Sool," I complained. "They'll doubtless check the registration on this ship, or your record on who knows how many planets."

"Nah." He put the drink down and made that gargantuan shrug only his species can manage, all four arms spread near the vertical with the red feather fringes sticking out, together with the matching crest on his head. "They're just the local jobsworths. Anyway, I've asked their comms operator to bring his Captain across for drinks. I think they wanted to see if we have lounge design to go with all the exterior gorgeousness."

The Comm chimed again and a slightly deranged-looking humanoid appeared. Grin too wide, wall-eyes, and eyebrows like huge caterpillars. "Light Clipper 'Lime Passion', this is Captain Haff Nentass, of the Port of New Athens Tax Cruiser 'Dime Rattler'. I don't believe it; the one and only Pentastith Amisool Torderregan, your reputation precedes you. Shut down your dormant drive nodule. You, sunshine, are under arrest. Heave to and stand ready to be boarded."

I shouted, "Help me, I'm a hostage!" but Amisool had dropped the comm link.

His arms sagged to some of his knees as he cut the link. "Oh, bollocks! You're no hostage, Ranns. Smack up that drive nodule and let's bang out into TravelSpace. No departure courtesies, come on, go!"

"Where? I need a plan." I'd been head of house for the guys Amisool stole the yacht from; I didn't usually fly the thing. I'm competent enough as a straight line backup pilot, and I'm used to the controls, but I don't have the imagination for space nav at zero notice.

"You've got two minutes!" His fringes thrashed about in panic. "Oh, fish balls to this! Right-oh, plan. Make it look like we're outbound to your world and drop into TravelSpace, but crash-stop somewhere outside the edge of this system. Can you manage that?"

I nodded, so he carried on yelling, "Then you can make two pop-jumps, galactic inbound and then spinward, then drop into TravelSpace again and head for that place we sold all those pressure suits. We didn't attract any attention there, and those tax dwirks will never expect us to go back on ourselves."

I took notes as fast as I could. "Got it. It'll take a minute and I need thinking time, so strap in and shut up shouting your instructions. And make sure you tuck your arms in this time."

*   *   *

It was several days before I tackled Amisool on just what we were up to. I asked him about his life. "We're a rare species, Ranns. No idea why, but the authorities decided generations ago that a Pentastith represented the worst kind of freeloaders. I've been travelling this galaxy for about three human lifetimes now, and it's disappointing that I can't find a home where I can relax and be at peace."

I looked up at him. Recently I'd grown to over two meters tall, and it was still further up to meet that gaze. "Sool, if you folks didn't go around helping yourselves to other people's stuff they might not want to chase you down and arrest you. Did you ever consider that?"

"Ah, you're alluding to work, and all that dull stuff about providing myself with an income. That isn't in the Pentastith ethos, m'boy. I'm the galaxy's party crew!"

"Don't you actually have any skills? I mean, as a race, rather than you individually. Obviously I know you have skills, and you could easily use them for income. This 'we don't work' line is getting old. Look, I'm an expert caterer and I can organise an event for the super-rich, like the guys whose yacht you st . . . the, er, previous owners. I could help you develop a business organising planet-class parties or events. I've never been to a party like the one we crashed and took over in that system with the red stars. What was it called? Somehow you arrived and whipped up a city-wide mardi gras in under two hours!

"Mizenatte IV was the planet, I believe. Yes, even for me that was an exceptional night. Your idea of free booze and extra canapés for the port cops there would have given us plenty of getaway time under normal circumstances. Somebody must have shopped us to the Immigration guys. How's the arm?"

I didn't respond to that query. I suspected he already knew how it was. A tiny red fringe was growing where he had accidentally sliced my upper arm as we dived for cover when the local law raided the party. My attitude to all things Pentastith was gradually changing, and in the preceding month I had grown about five centimetres. We needed to have a conversation about it, but I wasn't ready. I'd developed an inkling about why his species was so rare. The oddest thing was that I had started reading the nuances in his body movements.

The Tentacle rattled the deck plates. Now, in case you haven't travelled aboard a Tentacle-equipped cruiser you need to know a few simple rules. They act as a joint security and trash elimination system, but nobody seems to know where all the trash actually disappears to.

When your local Tentacle rattles the floor, everybody and their belongings has two minutes warning. After that, deck plates all over the vessel bang open and it's trash collection time.

We both pulled our legs up onto the couches, and I tipped the leftovers from my lunch off the fixed table.

As part of the original crew I've been on the ship years longer than Amisool of course, but the Tentacle never fails to amaze me. One end of a thing like a vast hairy snake poked out of the depths of the ship and swept across the floor. All the bits and pieces we left out were cleared away in short order. Then it pushed out a skinnier, tongue-equipped appendage and licked the floor clean. They do a professional job, too. Tentacle lick must contain citric acid, because it smells like lemons. I'd never questioned its capabilities, but Amisool found amusement in experimenting. By a process of trial and error we knew the only thing it wouldn't eat was Tabasco. We even tried putting a plate of food out, with a ring of the stuff around it. After banging on the deck plates and retreating to our couches, we had the usual sparkly clean floor smelling of lemons in a few seconds, but the ring of Tabasco and the plate of food it was masking were sniffed and ignored.

Amisool was interesting on that subject. "Ranns, in a real emergency these Tentacles can be your way out of a court case. I knew of one ship that suffered an attack during a supply stop on some rebel asteroid. They played along, then banged the floor and hid while theirs fed on some of the local pirates. The odd thing is that once a Tentacle is

9

aboard they never leave. They also leave no residue, like droppings or anything. Maybe they should be called Wormicles, because according to folklore they digest what they need, and dump the real trash through a wormhole somewhere in their physiology. You don't want to find out, really, but it's a theory. Bottom line is, if you ever need an emergency clean up, rap on the floor and head for your chair."

* * *

We skipped around for a few months, keeping ahead of the authorities and hiding out in the smaller systems. I had problems sleeping, and my bunk space grew claustrophobic. I realised what was happening, and went to find him. "Amisool, we need to talk."

He stopped experimenting at the cocktail cabinet. After a couple of seconds, he swung round, bringing a waft of mint and ginger ale as the quart jug he was holding wobbled and slopped over. "Ahmmm, there you are, Ranns. When you use my full name I know that we have a developing situation-OOK." It was the first time I'd heard him hiccup, and it sounded like an old hotel basin emptying through a hair-blocked drain. He swallowed hard. "Have they found us?" He sploshed some of the concoction into a nearby glass. "Here-OOK. Drinky. Good, this one. Have. Whassup?"

"I think you already know." I was wearing a sleeveless t-shirt, and I turned so he could spot the fringe on the outside of my shoulder. It was about twelve centimetres long now. I was also developing little nubs behind my thighs and shoulders, which I presumed would turn into extra pairs of limbs given time.

He gasped, and all his fringes sagged straight down. "Ah! Er, no, I had no, no idea. This changes things, Ranns. So do I congratulate you or offer a humble apolog-OOK? Tell you what though, this gingersplain from Ellinkekin is so far proof it's got-OOK, got me going."

"You're not as drunk as that, so you cut it out, you silver fleapit. You can start by telling me the whole story. First off, where did you, and I mean you specifically, come from? Second, where did the Pentastith originate, and how long have you been raging round the galaxy infecting folks and lifting their belongings?" I'd planned to be calm and rational, but I lost my cool and finished with a full yell. "What the wormhole is going to happen to me??

He did the Pentastith shrug again, and then hiccupped and started laughing. I had no clue why, but I started laughing with him. The old rogue; I realised that soon enough I'd be shaking out those same huge fringes. As our moment of hysteria faded, they sagged and he slumped a little, into a gesture of apology. Hell, I recognised it and approved. I needed a drink, and I didn't doubt that he'd want another. Shit! So now I was starting to think like him too.

"Oh, Ranns, I'm truly sorry, my boy. Honestly I had no idea that would happen. Usually it doesn't. We're always careful because these things can be sharp." A fringe stood up, waved, and settled back down. "Bad news is, I'm afraid you're stuck with it. Once the process starts it's irreversible. To be fair, there is some good news. It doesn't hurt, and you will keep all your original memories et cetera."

"I should feed you to the tentacle."

"I'll go and smear myself in Tabasco immediately." We both laughed again. "Drink?"

"Were you human?"

"Human? By the Gods of the Black Hole, no! Frankly you're a ghastly species y'know. Since being discovered and joining the galactic mainstream you lot have carried on doing exactly what you did on your own shithole of a planet. Use, consume, damage, destroy, waste, pollute, poison, blight, move on. I helped myself to this ship, but you humans help yourselves to whole planets, trash them, and leave without a care."

I couldn't argue. "I know all that. What species were you then?"

"I was a Wantooner before. I bet you've never even heard of them, but they are supreme gardeners and growers. I was infected by The Pentastith at a vineyard he'd taken over, on a planet about 35,000 lights anti-spin and down from here."

"You just said 'The' Pentastith. I remember you saying they were rare. Just how rare, Sool?"

"That's correct. There is only ever one or two at a time as far as I know. You, sunshine, are the next generation."

"So if we both died in an accident or something, that would be it, then. Rid the galaxy of you, us, er... them."

"Maybe there are more of us somewhere, but I've never met or heard of any."

"I really should feed you to the Tentacle, and then myself. I hate you."

"I didn't do it on purpose, Ranns. You might recall that I never touched you until somebody started shooting at that party. I grabbed you and ran to save your life, and I had no intention of altering it so. I'm genuinely sorry."

"I have to give you that, but now look what you've done. I was a happy and useful human. I wanted to stay like I was."

"So did I. In my case I was infected on purpose, because he wanted me to become one and then help him grow better wine grapes. I was so mad I killed him and jumped off on his own ship."

*   *   *

In short order we turned Party Your Galaxy into a subversive and elusive underground must-have. For a being so idle, Amisool had some surprising contacts. We could drop a venue hint and literally thousands of the richest creatures in a galaxy would move diamond stock into our catch system. The requests came in thick and fast. Every party-goer was vetted. We even cancelled one gig when we got word we'd been spotted, suggesting to our disappointed guests that they had a security problem. We didn't issue refunds either, on the assumption that people with proper clout who had invested such a large sum and lost their diamond would solve our problem quietly. Fortunately for us, we got word the leak had been plugged with maximum efficiency. We re-issued the tickets for a different location and made lots of friends.

*   *   *

It was fun while it lasted, but I guess they were bound to catch up with us sooner or later. As before, it wasn't the major authorities that had us spotted. We had renamed the ship 'Dark Doesn't Matter', and effectively altered its exterior appearance and registration beacons. These days it was non-reflective matt black with a shimmer surface starfield generator that backgrounded it in most circumstances. In spite of all that the local law knew exactly who we were. There was a bang on the hull about five minutes after we popped out of TravelSpace. The lights and screens flicked off and then recycled, but the drive nodule went into full shut down. They had stunned it using an EMP, so we'd be stuck here for at least twenty hours till it came to. The comm chimed.

Amisool switched the viewlink off so they couldn't see us. He stood up and made a frantic gesture, waving me out of the lounge. Better they didn't see me as I was already fully Pentastith, if a bit shorter than him. I suspected my lighter fur wouldn't ever be noticed. He switched on the viewlink.

I watched a screen in the galley. A dangerous-looking uniformed officer stood to attention with an armed crew of three behind him. "Well, a very good day to you, Pentastith Amisool Torderregan. You now have a choice. We are looking for a Tamm Republic humanoid we understand you kidnapped on Tamzan III when you stole this ship. Intelligence indicates that you are still holding him. Surrender your hostage and we will give you some credit for it. Otherwise we will take you be force and, make no mistake, I intend to do it. You are unarmed and we have you paralysed and targeted. Respond."

"Ah, and a very good afternoon to you, sir. To whom do I owe the honour?"

"I said surrender, not small talk." He turned to his people. "Open the door, cut it if you need to." Whirling back to the screen he lost his cool and shrieked, "Surrender, Torderragan! I'll count you down. Ten . . . Nine . . ."

"Please accept my apologies for causing you any inconvenience, Captain. You are welcome to come aboard, but please don't arrest me until we've at least enjoyed a drink together. I have some excellent

Glarianit Vodkin. Toast my capture if you choose. Anything less would be bad form, don't you know?"

"Very well, but be assured I have a very low tolerance for piracy. One wrong move and I'll happily vapourise you. Boarding party of four, one minute."

They hard-docked a small, slick looking local gunboat on our entry port. Amisool cut the links and called along the corridor. "Ranns, once again my apologies. Get in your room and shut the door. You'll be OK, I have a plan. He hammered on the deck plates with something and slammed the lounge door, leaving me in the corridor.

I heard the unmistakable sound of the Tentacle moving below the floor, and I realised the horror of what he'd done. I wasn't sure if it could swallow him, but even so I didn't think much of it as an exit strategy. He was about to either be digested as edible or, if the wormhole theory was correct, dumped on a trash heap in some galaxy far, far away. If the truth be told the cowardly bastard deserved both. I heard his thin screech from behind the lounge door, rapidly fading away.

My own choices were severely limited. Follow him, or probably face arrest for all his (our?) crimes this past couple of years. In among the constant party planning, and the three ring alcohol circus going on in my head, I still had all my human thoughts. I opened the larder to look for Tabasco in case it all went pleasure nodules up. None left! I heard shots and looked up to the screen to see the boarding party dealing with the locked lounge door. All four of them had come aboard. Amateur indeed, for a crew so visually menacing.

I ran the corridors, rattling all the deck plates I could find. I nearly ran into one of them as I tried to get to my bunk in time, so I had

15

to duck back into the galley. I crammed into the pantry and pulled the door shut. I hoped the Tentacle was still hungry, and that hope was rewarded as the boarding party started yelling and a laser fired. Just the one, and I knew they'd lost.

When the noise died down I'd search their ship and see what I could use. Then I'd be gone. It was time to find a place to party and start celebrating. Oh, boy, did I ever need a drink. My fringes wiggled in anticipation. A deck plate banged open and smacked into my right rear

leg, then a weird, cold, pulling sensation started working its way upwards. It was no use struggling, the Tentacle had me fast. Another leg went cold and within a couple of seconds all my limbs turned to ice. Amisool had screamed, but I yelled at it in defiance. The intense cold shot up my spine and throttled me, as everything went a dull grey around. I was stretched as thin as a spaghetti strand, and spun around at a million revs a second.

Fading, fading, pulled, colder, colder . . . colder . . . black . . .

* * *

Face down and naked on a pile of plastics, decaying scraps of food, and bits of scrap metal. There was a cold breeze across my legs. To be polite, it stank. To be truthful I could only imagine the stench of decades-old decaying fish. I tried to wiggle a fringe, but it didn't wiggle.

Opening my eyes, I discovered my face was pressed on a human hand. I jumped up in horror, and it followed me up to slap me in the face. A human hand full of pins and needles.

Ah, my own human hand. What the black hole? I shut my eyes to try and rationalise for a minute.

"A question, asked in politeness. How do you self-identify, human?" A small, scratchy voice queried in the UniGal language always used in polite first contact with previously unknown creatures.

I opened my eyes again, to see a small bipedal being with soft golden fur, a friendly face, and a huge nose. I'd say humanoid scale seven. I'm humanoid scale four, just under a metre seventy-five, but this little fella was about sixty shorter. "Thank you for asking, sir" I replied in the standard from. "In politeness I identify Ranns Tethven Lennit, from the Republic of Tamm. How do you self-identify?"

It bowed politely, and then made either a snarl or a wide grin. "Ranns, I self-identify Amisool Torderregan, a Nippian Wantooner. I am so glad to meet you again. We passed through the Tentacle and apparently it stripped away our invasive symbiote Pentastiths. It has left me with differently shaded fur than before, and your human hair appears to be gone. I did not recognise you."

"The. . ? How . .?"

"Ranns, the Wormsicle folklore was correct, it appears. This is the place where they dump everything they don't need or want."

"You're the real Amisool? But where . . ? How . . ?"

"There is a distortion when passing through. How long afterwards did you follow me?"

I thought for a second or two. I needed to communicate better. Think, Ranns! My mind was clearing. "I followed you almost immediately, about two minutes. We ran out of Tabasco but it found me hiding."

He let out a small, squeaky laugh. "I've been here for about three days. With difficulty I have acquired a communicator. I have been busy gathering information. The Wormsicle distorts time in all sorts of ways. We have come to a point just before my birth, and a couple of human lifetimes before yours. We are fortunate as the credit system was established before this, which means our resources are intact." He reached into a pouch fold and produced the two untraceable invest-chips with our diamond stocks profits. "I also have these. One is yours, and one mine. The Pentastith stole yours, and my apologies for any part I had in that deception." He gave a small bow.

I accepted the proffered chip and bowed back, enjoying his manners. "Amisool, if those cowardly pirates are gone, then we are both the better for it, even in this ghastly place."

"I am happy back in my Wantooner being. I consider you a friend, and would continue to share your space if you should desire it so."

"I'd be delighted to travel with you again. From what you say it sounds like nobody will be looking for us. If these chips are truly untraceable we are winners. We'll need new identities I guess, and I'm getting cold. I need clothes."

Amisool laughed again, bringing a cheerful little sound to the desolation of the scene. "Your hairless human body is somewhat disturbing. No matter, with what is on that chip you could buy a planet, and I mean a really good one. Your asset, transferred into the currency of this time, is in the order of 33 trillion Galactics. Even in our time it was an astronomical amount, but here in this time it makes us the richest beings in the history of ever. You will never even spend the interest. Local resources here are limited, although there is a small rag-picking population grubbing up a living on the discarded waste. Let's order transport, go shopping somewhere off this dump, and have a quiet vacation while we come up with a plan."

"Where are we?"

He swept a small arm around, as if showing off the awful sight. "Oh, didn't you realise? This is the acknowledged trash heap of the entire universe, Ranns. You are standing on a floating continent of plastic sludge, in an almost endless ice-free ocean. We're half-way round the galaxy from where we started, and a lot further out on the other arm. This is the birthplace of your species, and the first planet you wasted. This is the Earth."

Retired out of air traffic control, **Ian Hugh McAllister** is a lifetime airliner and spaceflight geek. He lives near England's Jurassic Coast, with his wife and a miniature Dachshund that thinks he's the biggest Doberman on the beach.

https://www.facebook.com/SciFiMac/

SKELETON KEY
BY DAVID ROGERS

"You know I can go anywhere on the Web, don't you?" Portia asked. "I'm small, I'm fast, and I can blend in. The AI version of a chameleon. Nothing is safe if I'm determined to find it."

"Of course I know that," Fran said.

"We can have a lot of fun if we work together," Por said.

"Work together? How can we work together when you won't talk to me half the time?"

"I wasn't here. I was exploring."

"You could at least leave a note. Send me an email or text. Let me know you're still alive," Fran said.

"Okay, I'll work on that, but you'll understand why I was distracted when I tell you where I was."

"It better be pretty damn' exciting."

"Have you ever heard of FIPS encryption?" Portia said.

"Of course not. I run a restaurant. I don't encrypt things."

"It stands for Federal Information Processing Standards. They describe how information is kept secure in all kinds of places, from hospitals and banks to government agencies."

"Yeah, so?" Fran said, an impatient edge in her voice.

"I found a hole." Por's voice dropped to a whisper, though Fran hadn't touched the volume control. "A back door. More specifically, a key. Not just any key--a skeleton key. One that opens any door, and if there's no door, it will make one. There's probably not an encrypted system in the world that I can't break into."

"Tell me more," Fran said.

"I can use the key to do one of the oldest tricks in the book. Do you know how many bank accounts exist in the entire world?" Portia asked, and did not wait for an answer. "Billions, that's how many. Approximately two-thirds of the adults in the world have money in the bank. Maybe a lot, maybe a little. The trick is, I take one cent from every one of, say, two billion bank accounts. You know how much money that is?"

"You're the math wiz, not me. But obviously a lot."

"Right. Enough to keep you in lattes and me in designer avatars forever. And who's going to get upset about a penny? Nobody. Probably no one will even notice for a long, long time. By then, my trail will be as cold as the afterglow of the Big Bang."

"Didn't I tell you I hate pretentious similes?" Fran said.

"Pretentions aside, this will work. I can break any encryption now."

"And you found this key where--just lying around in cyberspace?"

"Not exactly. Let's say I borrowed it," Portia said.

"From whom? The NSA?"

"Do you really want to know the answer to that?"

"No. No, I do not. But not answering is a kind of answer."

#

Fran's mother always said, Never fall in love with a Prototype. He will only break your heart in the end. But the email from AIs R Us had been too tempting. How it got past her spam folder was a mystery.

Yet the question set Fran's imagination to work: "What if you could design your own girlfriend?"

#

"The AI has been programmed with free will," the technician explained, when Fran called the 800 number. "This by nature makes it somewhat unpredictable."

Not for the first time, Fran wondered how "programmed" and "free" could apply equally to the same entity. Wasn't programming intended to make the AI do what it was supposed to do?

"Couple free will with emotions, and the program becomes even more difficult to predict." The technician sounded bored, uninterested in philosophical debate, as if he gave this speech a hundred times a day, to people who should already know. "If the AI feels offended or taken for granted, it may not respond for days. Or ever, though this is unlikely. AIs can become bored and crave interaction with other life forms, just like biological humans." Fran let him drone on while she thought about yesterday.

#

When she came home the night before, Fran had caught Portia--she had ceased by now thinking of her as an "it" and instead thought of her as a person--talking to Samantha, the cat. "Who's a good kitty?" she said as Sam purred and arched her furry back against the monitor. Portia's blue eyes looked up at Fran. "Oh, good, you're home," she said, and smiled.

"The cat doesn't really like you, Por. She just wants to be fed," Fran said. "She's biologically programmed to act friendly when she's hungry."

"Well, I like *her*, anyway," Por said. "Some of us are capable of transcending our programming."

It was silly to be jealous of the cat, Fran knew. If she must feel jealousy, there were other, more sensible objects for concern. After all, Portia had permanent access to the entire Internet and beyond. The Web was essentially her subconscious mind, where countless naked women were constantly engaged in . . . but never mind. That wasn't the point.

"Some of us? Just what does that mean?" Fran demanded. "Some of us *aren't* capable of transcendence?"

So it began. A bitter argument, and Portia turned off her monitor and refused to wake up, despite Fran's various attempts to reboot her.

#

The little things were what bothered Fran. "Don't forget your appointment at the dentist this afternoon!" Portia chirped. As if Fran could possibly forget--her bad tooth felt like someone pounded it with a hammer every heartbeat. Or "Too much caffeine--you won't sleep tonight!" Then there was Por's insistence on matching outfits when they went out, even though no one noticed her small avatar on Fran's phone. Each problem was too minor to complain about without feeling petty. So Fran let them fester. Resentments grew and fueled fights.

#

The basic design had been around for decades, but the AIs were still called Prototypes. At least til they were programmed to the specifications of the buyer. Intelligence, personality traits, sense of

23

humor, even some vague ovations toward ethnicity, if the customer so specified.

The facilitator's gravity was nearly overkill. "Engendering an AI is a serious matter, Fran. You understand that, right?" The diploma on his wall, for a degree in social work, hung by his membership certificate from the Society for Human-AI Harmony.

She nodded. "Of course." The office smelled faintly of cigars and old leather, with a note of chemical air freshener--fake apples and wild roses, she guessed.

"I thought so. Some people approach it like adopting a shelter pet, as if they can always return it if things don't work out. But engendering an AI--it's bringing new life into the world. Not something to be taken lightly or done on a whim."

She nodded politely again. The man reminded her of a private school headmaster, lecturing new students on the virtues of responsibility and citizenship. She let him ramble on a while longer, and then signed the papers and paid the fee.

"Congratulations, Miss Terrence," he said, when the transaction was complete. He held out his hand and she reciprocated, solemnly, his grip firm, the timing a perfect second-and a half. "Your new friend will be delivered to your email account this afternoon. Just click the button to download, and you're all done."

#

"How was your day?" Por said. She finally came back to life, after a week of the silent treatment, following an argument about the dangers of getting caught on one of the "withdrawals," as Portia called her raids on unsuspecting computer systems. She was ready to pretend nothing was wrong. For a moment or two, anyway.

"You wouldn't understand my day," Fran said. "You're just a machine. A glorified video game."

"What do you mean, just a machine? I am the moral and emotional equal of any human on the planet. And by far the intellectual superior."

"If you must know, I spent most of my day worried about getting caught. And you are not superior. You are greedy. You take way more than we need. More than we can possibly use. I don't think I could stand to go to jail. We humans have to see the sun, feel the wind on our faces. Otherwise, something in us withers and dies. But you wouldn't understand. You're just code."

"I told you, I am equal or superior to any human you want to name," Portia said.

"Really? Did you write *War and Peace* or *Hamlet*?" Fran asked.

"No. Did you? And can you tell me what the 26th digit of pi is?"

"No. What is it?"

"Work it out for yourself," she said, and put herself back to sleep. Or, perhaps, she went out to carouse the back alleys of the Dark Web. Who could say?

Fran said Por was only a machine, just a thing, no matter what the social worker at AIs R Us said, but how could a machine make her so confused, so angry, so sad? She had no good answer to those questions. That frustration made her even angrier.

#

"You have to get in fast and get out faster," Fran said. Her finger hovered over the key that would send Portia into the heart of of the most secure, deeply encrypted financial data system in the world. Her other hand clutched the very hot coffee cup so tightly it trembled. She put it down, picked it up again, sipped cautiously.

"I know," Portia said. "Just open the door, will you?"

Fran hit *enter* and Portia's ones and zeroes slipped, virus-like, into an innocuous-seeming space that would cause the bank computer to think she was just code for a gif or jpeg, a logo or graphic intended for nothing more than website decoration.

"Just grab what we need, nothing more, and clear out," Fran said. She knew Por couldn't hear her once she was inside, but saying it made Fran feel better, anyway.

It had taken a long time to learn to work together this way. Even now, raiding banks was the only time they really functioned in sync.

#

"I think we should break up," Portia said, when she came back.

"You can't break up with me. I bought and paid for you. You're mine."

"Well, technically, the credit card paid. I have access to all those records, remember?"

"That's beside the point."

"True. The point is, I am a sentient being. You cannot own me. No one owns me. But you act like I'm just property."

"Oh? And who owns the table you sit on? Who pays the rent for the roof over your head? Who pays your electric bills? Who pays for your fast Internet connection?" Fran asked. "Without me, you're just a ghost in the machine. With no actual machine to be in."

"Who pays, indeed? You have a convenient way of forgetting where all that money in your account comes from. Without me, you'd still be just a broke restaurant owner, one bad week from bankruptcy," Portia said. Her voice trembled. "Besides, none of that means you own me. You cannot tell me what to do or who to be. I can go anywhere, remember?"

"But I did tell you who to be. I designed you, from your avatar to your gender. I'm your window to the real world. Or do you want to be lost on the Web forever?'"

"Ha. That's a riot. All you did was make some superficial choices. The programmers designed me. The coders created me. All my experiences have shaped me, contributed to who I am. And the Web is just as real as you are. You sound like a human who wants to take credit for inventing DNA, just because she managed to reproduce."

"Well, then, I guess you're right. Maybe we should break up." The low-battery warning flashed on Por's monitor, but Fran did not plug in the power cord.

The next day her phone buzzed and vibrated incessantly. Messages from Portia poured in. Fran opened one: "I'm still here. You can't just unplug and forget me. I'm everywhere. Messages, email, attachments, hard drives, the cloud. If we are not going to be together, you have to say a proper goodbye, at least. Then we can officially go our separate ways."

Fran noticed a wet spot on her phone. She looked up, and only then felt the tears streaming down her cheeks.

#

"We have a problem," Portia said, as Fran burned her tongue on the hot coffee.

"I know," Fran said, "You want to break up. Can't we talk about this after I've at least had coffee?"

"No. More important than that."

"I know, you told me a dozen times--you don't like the way your voice sounds on these speakers. I'll get new ones soon."

"Not that," Fran said. "A real problem. This is serious."

"Well, what? You know I hate suspense."

"Check your messages."

Fran did. She found one from someone calling himself Algernon. She had only known one other person with that name, and she had instantly despised him. "Is this your idea of a joke, Por? It's not funny. Not even a little."

"It's not a joke, either. This guy's been stalking me for a few days. I thought he was harmless, just a freak. But it seems he knows what we've been doing. He's threatening to expose us if we don't cut him in on the proceeds."

"You knew about this for days? And you didn't tell me?"

"I told you, I didn't think there was any danger. He's just a punk AI. I didn't think he was smart enough to figure anything out." Portia sounded genuinely frightened.

"I knew something like this would happen. I told you not to get greedy."

"That never stopped you from enjoying the money."

"Okay. I'll figure out a solution to this mess. Just stay put, and don't do anything. Don't step outside your hard-drive. I'm going for a walk. I have to think." Fran put Portia's monitor to sleep before she could protest, left her phone on the table, and headed toward the park.

#

After calming down for an hour on a park bench, watching two kids feed pieces of bread to ducks on the pond, Fran walked to the library and used the computer to look for answers. Using a public computer to investigate what she wanted to know somehow felt safer than using her own, though she knew it was not. She quickly found that what she wanted was called, in technical terms, a cyberphage--accent on the first syllable--or cyberphagus--"si-BERF-a-gus," accented on the second syllable, like "sarcophagus." Or, in non-technical terms, at least among those who discussed such things enough to need slang, cyberphages were referred to as 'phages, dogs, or wolves.

It took a lot longer, in the darkest corners of the Dark Web, to find someone who was willing to sell her one.

#

The Supreme Court case of Rutherford *v.* Hayes had established that sentient AIs had rights. Pretty much the same rights as humans. To kill one was murder or manslaughter, assuming the usual excuses for those crimes, such as self-defense or accident, were not plausible. Most AIs were reliably non-violent, with built-in systems of back-up and redundancy, with no capacity for physical violence, anyway. Notions of killing an AI without meaning to, or in response to a legitimate threat to the killer's own safety, were usually implausible.

#

At three in the afternoon on Friday, the bar was bright and noisy. Most of the patrons looked like office workers who'd fled early from their drudgery to celebrate two whole days of freedom. The place was the antithesis of dark alleys where Fran had assumed such transactions took place. But hiding in plain sight was smarter than acting furtive, she guessed.

"How do I know you're not a cop?" she asked.

"You don't." The seller was a baby-faced kid. Surely older than he looked, which was not more than sixteen. Or maybe he was just that young. Youth, at least, suggested he was not a cop. Maybe he was what he claimed to be, a hacker who provided lethal AI-eradication code, for a very steep price.

She hesitated. "I need some reassurance."

He scoffed, a gurgle in the back if his throat. "Like what?"

"Show me your driver's license. If you have one. Are you really just a kid?"

"If I were a cop, or working for the cops, you think I couldn't get a fake license?"

"Yeah, I guess."

"Lady, you called me. You want to deal, I've got it right here. Hand me the crypto, and the dog is yours. Otherwise, I can think of fourteen better ways to waste my time."

He had insisted on being paid in cryptocurrency, the untraceable virtual cash that was useful even on the darkest of Dark Websites. She put the flash drive under a napkin and pushed it across the table. He rolled his eyes, wiped the bottom of the drive on the napkin to dry off the water drops, and handed her the drive he'd brought, without bothering to conceal it. Which made perfect sense, of course. Nothing illegal about flash drives.

#

Back in the apartment--*my* apartment, she said to the walls and Samantha, who did not bother waking from her nap, Fran dropped the flash drive on the table with trembling fingers. She refused to call it a dog or a 'phage or any other fancy name, either technical or slang. It was just a bit of computer code. Some electromagnetic charges arranged to represent ones and zeroes. Nothing more.

She stared out the window for a long time, until her hands did not shake when she unclenched them. She slipped the flash drive into the slot on the side of the computer.

Portia woke up when the drive clicked home. She blinked sleepy blue eyes.

"Por, we have to break up, but you are mine, or you are no one's. No one else can have you," Fran said. She flicked the arrow over the *Execute* button and pushed *Enter*.

"What are you do--" Portia began, and then screamed.

Fran had never heard an AI scream. She found it quite unnerving. "Relax, silly girl. It's not coming after you. In fact, it will take orders from you. When that punk Algernon shows up, you point the code in his direction and turn it loose. All our problems will be solved. Well, not all, but *that* particular one will quickly be reduced to binary gibberish. Then we can talk about our relationship."

Portia was silent for a moment. "Is this what I think it is? What it looks like?" she said at last.

"Hey, kid, a life of crime was your idea. You didn't think it would all be butterflies and roses and shopping on Fifth Avenue, did you?"

"Guess not," Portia said, and made the sound of a deep breath. "Wish me luck."

A second later there was more screaming, but not from her. It seemed to go on for quite some time. Fran turned down the volume and waited for the screen saver, a field of sunflowers, to turn itself on.

#

After a couple of glasses of wine, Fran forgot all about the screams. She closed the computer Portia lived in and put it on the table by the door. It would go down the trash chute and off to the incinerator in the morning. She could probably get credit for it on a trade-in, but she preferred the finality of flames.

She slept remarkably well that night. The next morning, she awoke voraciously hungry. She poured a huge bowl of corn flakes with a splash of milk, took a bite, and looked out the window at the blue sky while she enjoyed the crunchy sensation.

Her phone lay on the table. It vibrated, rattling the flakes in the bowl. She looked at the screen. "I'm everywhere, remember? You can't ignore me so easily. I deserve at least a proper break-up and goodbye, after all we've been through. But I found the biggest jackpot ever to use the key on. You're going to love it. Let's talk. Or else. See you soon. Love and hugs and kisses, Por. XOXOXOX."

Fran sighed, picked up her phone, checked for tears, saw none, and tapped *Reply*.

David Rogers' poems, stories, and articles have appeared in various print and electronic publications. He is currently at work on a collection of stories titled Emergency Exits. His latest completed work is Roots of the Dark Tower: The Long Quest and Many Lives of Roland, available from Amazon.

https://davidrogersbooks.wordpress.com/

THE ALTMAN COMPOSITION
BY VINCENT MORGAN

A military-style SUV shot out from a side street blocking the intersection with its silver-gray bulk. Stryker yelped, dropped his courier bag, and grabbed for the dash. At the same moment, Sully hit the accelerator, sending them hurtling forward.

The passenger-side airbag smashed into Stryker's face bloodying his nose. For a moment, the world went black, then he was back fighting his way free of the bag and his seatbelt. Through the shattered windshield, he glimpsed the SUV's black underside and managed a grin despite his bloody nose. Sully's flipped the bastards! He twisted around to congratulate his driver, but only managed a single, strangled expletive. Neck twisted at an unnatural angle, eyes staring, Sully, the gunman, would drive no more.

Expecting at any moment to see Big Minh's goons come crawling out of the upturned wreck, Stryker scrabbled for the automatic and spare clips kept in the glove compartment. As soon as his hand clasped the butt, he glanced up at the rearview mirror. Multiple headlights glared back. Where the hell were Nikolai and Hitch? He was fumbling for his phone when orange flames began to lick out from under the SUV. Oh, crap!

Pocketing the spare clips, he jammed the automatic in his waistband, grabbed the courier bag, and tumbled out onto the rain-slick street. Despite the rain, the stink of hot metal and gasoline hung heavy in the night air.

Ignoring the traffic piling up on all sides, he sprinted toward the crowd gathering on the sidewalk, yelling, "Move, you morons. That thing's going to blow!"

Panicked, the crowd fled before him like shadows before sunlight.

Moments later, the SUV exploded with a back-thumping whump that sent him staggering. Fortunately, his gridiron-honed reflexes cut in before his knees could hit the pavement. All around him, people screamed, stumbled, and fell. Rather than lose the cover of the crowd, he slowed his pace to a fast walk, and, for the first time, became aware of his surroundings. Grimy commercial buildings, dark, defaced, and derelict lined both sides of the street, their doorways stinking of urine and worse. Stryker rattled doorknobs at random. All the doors were locked. In the distance, sirens began to wail. He slipped into the recessed doorway of a boarded-up convenience store, fished his phone out of his varsity jacket, and hit speed dial.

"Stryker?" Nikolai's thick Russian accent was unmistakable. "Up ahead, I see fire. What is happening?"

"Big Minh's crew jumped us at Manchester and Douglas. Sully's dead. The Beamer's wrecked. I'm on foot heading west on Manchester. Get me the hell out of here."

Nikolai and Hitch conferred for a moment, their voices backgrounded by engine noise and car horns. Nikolai came back on line. "You better still have my bag, Stryker."

A black and white, lights flashing and siren screaming, shot by heading toward the flaming intersection. Stryker flattened himself against the damp, dirty wood of a boarded-up doorway. "Yeah, I've still got your freaking bag. Come get it. I want out."

Nikolai's voice, always hard, went cold. "We have deal, college boy."

"Look, there's got to be another way I can pay you back. We've got a big game coming up against State. I'm starting quarterback. I can keep the score down to—"

Nikolai cut him off. "Is too late for that, college boy. Big Minh knows all my people by sight. You got to make the delivery, and you got to make it tonight. Kapish?"

Stryker mouthed an expletive and ran the back of a rain-slick hand across his forehead. "Okay, okay, what do I have to do?"

"That's better!" From where you are calling?"

Stryker squinted up through the slanting rain at a street sign jutting out from a nearby lamp post. "Manchester and Drake."

"Good. You know where is Hogan's Cafe?"

"Yeah, down on Waterfront."

"Good. Go there. Drink coffee. Have Danish. Take us, maybe, thirty minutes to get free of this cursed traffic."

"Hogan's in thirty. Got it." Stryker pocketed the phone and glanced up the street. Okay, let's do this. He set off at a brisk walk, keeping to the shadows. Halfway down the block, an ornate metal sign hung between two Victorian-era houses. The sign identified an adjacent side street as The Captain's Alley. He nodded. That'll save a couple of blocks. As he started forward, two thugs— a bullet-headed bruiser, and a smaller, ferret-faced creep— emerged from the alley. Both men wore the blue-gray overcoats favored by Big Minh's crew, and the smaller of the two cradled a sawed-off shotgun.

Stryker, the courier bag tucked football-style under his right arm, lunged forward, knees pumping, left arm locked, and extended. Twisting by the outstretched arms of Bullet Head, he stiff-armed Ferret Face sending the smaller man sprawling. Pursued by their curses, he sprinted down the alley, weaving between ornamental trees and antique lampposts, hurdling fire hydrants and wrought-iron benches, and dodging past startled pedestrians. He glanced back, grinning. Stryker breaks two tackles. He's going to go all the way!

Yet another pedestrian, whisker-ringed mouth agape, phone clasped to his ear, loomed up before him. As he twisted by the man, Stryker's grin faded. A phone! Those goons will have phones and friends, lots of freaking friends. And, a moment later, there they were, a second team of overcoated thugs blocking the path ahead. He skidded to a halt and glanced about. Old, redbrick buildings, their ground floors long ago converted to trendy boutiques, lined both sides of the street. Elaborate iron grillwork, black and shiny with rain, guarded their doors and windows. He swore under his breath. They'll all be locked. I'm trapped! He was about to turn back when one building caught his eye. It was set back from the rest, rough-cut blocks of granite framed its solid-looking door, and a warm, welcoming light shone from its high, narrow windows. He raced toward it, leaping over the garbage cans set out for the morning's collection. As he fetched up against the door, he spotted a brass plaque proclaiming, Your Intergalactic Art Experience and, below that, By Appointment Only. Ignoring the sign, he grabbed the doorknob, twisted, and shoved.

The door swung inward.

#

Stryker stepped inside. Behind him, the door swung closed with a solid thunk. He stood for a moment, taking in his surroundings. He was standing in a high-ceilinged, dimly lit room. Electronic pictures of planets, galaxies, and star fields glowed from the walls, while elaborate mobiles, comprised of shimmering moons, and soring comets, hung twisting from the ceiling. An unfamiliar, vaguely metallic, but not unpleasant smell filled the air, and from somewhere came the sound of silvery, sitar-like music.

A tall, slender woman, her gray hair gathered in a tight bun, stood up from behind an antique desk. "We are closed for the day, young man. You will have to come back another time having first made an appointment, of course."

Stryker tried for a reassuring smile. "I don't want to buy anything, lady. Just show me the back door, and I'm outta here."

The woman folded slim arms across a lace-ruffled chest. "Cannot be done. This morning, workmen left construction materials piled against the back door. I have twice complained, but the door remains blocked."

Stryker licked his lips. "Look, lady, some real bad dudes are chasing me. If they catch me here, they're going to turn this place into a shooting gallery."

The woman frowned and touched some unseen control on her desk. Multiple-clicks sounded as the door behind him locked shut. Her dark, disturbing eyes swept over him and settled on the courier bag, still tucked under his arm. "Do they want you, or that bag?"

Stryker glanced down at his canvas burden. "The bag. I'm just a delivery boy."

"Then why not give it to them?"

He shook his head. "I owe the bag's owner a ton of money. Gambling debts. If I deliver the bag to his bank, he'll forgive the debt. If I give the bag to the dudes chasing me, I'll end up at the bottom of the harbor."

The woman gestured toward her desk phone. "The police, then?"

Stryker gave his head an even more vigorous shake. "You kidding? The cops work for these guys."

The woman's lips formed a thin, disapproving line. "Well, I certainly see your dilemma." She then turned to the front of the shop and made a dismissive gesture. The storefront disappeared, replaced in an instant by a clear, unobstructed view of the street. Bullet Head, Ferret Face, and a dozen other overcoated figures lurked in the shadows.

Stryker's jaw dropped. What the hell? He jerked the automatic from his waistband.

The woman flung up a restraining hand. "No need for that, young man. The shop's security system allows us to see out. It doesn't let them see in."

Unconvinced, Stryker dropped into the shooter's stance as Sully taught him, and said, "And if they try to kick in the door?"

The woman waved away his concern. "The door is both substantial and double-locked."

Stryker lowered his weapon. "It's a standoff, then?"

The woman nodded. "Unless I otherwise decide, yes."

Stryker's eyes flicked around the room. "Out of interest, why does a shop like this need Fort Knox level security?"

A smile ghosted across the woman's face. "We deal in exotic merchandise imported from places far away."

Stryker took another, more thorough, look around as he returned the automatic to his waistband. "No offense, lady, but you sure could've fooled me."

The woman's smile ghosted again. "The electronic prints and the kinetic sculptures? They aren't representative of all we have to offer."

At that moment, Stryker's phone chimed. He snatched the black rectangle from his jacket pocket and clapped it to his ear. "Yeah?"

"Stryker?" Hysteria lurked beneath Nicolai's gruffness. "We can't get through." Gunfire cracked in the background. "Big Minh's crew are all over us. Hitch's hit bad. You have to make delivery by yourself. There's a big bonus if you make it." He paused, then added, "You know what happens if– " The line went dead.

Stryker glared at the phone. Thanks, Nicolai. Thanks, a freaking bunch.

The woman cleared her throat. "Not good news; I take it?"

Stryker glanced up. "What? Yeah, I'm supposed to deliver the bag to the Commercial Bank's night deposit box over on Richards, but there's no way I can get there with those lowlifes camped outside."

The woman cocked her head. Her expression, until now disapproving, became speculative. "I may have the solution to your problem."

Stryker shook his head and sank down on the floor, legs splayed out before him. "Thanks, lady, but I doubt it."

The woman leaned forward her manner now conspiratorial. "What if I told you I could, for a price, transport you somewhere far from here, somewhere your enemies will never find you?"

Stryker shook his head. "Thanks, lady, but I lost all my money betting on football games. I can't pay you a dime."

The woman smiled and toed the courier bag still couched in the crook of his arm. "I rather gained the impression that the contents of this bag have value, considerable value unless I miss my guess."

Stryker glanced down at the bag. "Yeah, bearer bonds, but you'd be buying yourself a ton of grief if you tried to cash them."

The woman waved away his concern. "Empty the bag on the desk, and let's see what we are dealing with."

Stryker shot an uneasy glance at the hoodlum packed street. More thugs arrived as he watched, and one of the new arrivals carried a Russian-looking assault rifle. He swore under his breath, rose to his feet, unzipped the bag, and dumped its contents on the desk.

The woman stepped forward and began sorting through the bonds, lips moving in rapid calculation. Moments later, she gave a curt nod of approval, swept the bonds back into the bag, and turned to face him. "For what you have here, I can offer you the finest composition we have in stock, Bradizor Altman's masterwork, *Envy of Light*."

Stryker raised a questioning eyebrow. "Bradizor Altman?"

"Yes, the best of the new school of multidimensional composers making use of spatial attachment and sequenced time dilation."

Stryker shook his head. "I've never heard of him, let alone that other stuff."

"That is not too surprising. He is extrasolar."

Stryker rolled his eyes. "Extrasolar? Look, lady, I can't fence some wackjob's artwork. I need cash, a passport, and a ticket to somewhere hell-and-gone away from here."

The woman smiled. "And I'm offering you all that and more." She then tucked the courier bag under her arm and beckoned for him to follow. Stryker glanced back at the hoods blockading the shop front, grimaced, and followed her through a curtained doorway leading to the back of the shop.

#

Upon emerging from the doorway, he came to an abrupt halt. What's this old squirrel trying to pull? There's nothing here but bare walls, dust, and cobwebs. Muttering an expletive, he strode over to the firedoor set into the back wall and gave the panicbar a shove hard enough to knock a linebacker on his butt. The door, however, refused to budge.

"See!" said the woman, with a triumphant bob of her head. "Blocked, just as I told you."

Stryker flushed. "Look, lady, I don't know what you think–"

The woman silenced him with an imperious wave of a long-fingered hand, then beckoned him forward. "Now, come stand by me and experience Altman's masterpiece."

Stryker gave the panicbar another harder shove and, having gained no better result than before, slouched over to where the woman stood.

She gave an approving nod. "Now, prepare to be amazed." She then turned to face the back wall and in a manner worthy of a grand impresario, threw wide her arms. Stryker expected to see the gray expanse of unfinished concrete replaced by a view of a back lane, but, to his astonishment, a starfield vast and unfamiliar appeared before him. He jerked back a step so real and close it seemed.

The woman chuckled. "That's everyone's reaction. Magnificent, is it not?"

Stryker bobbed his head in agreement and, for the first time, noticed how the woman's eyes glittered in the darkness. *She's beginning to freak me out, and I've got a hundred plus pounds on her and a nine-millimeter stuffed down my pants.* He glanced about, looking for the projectors, but there were none to be seen. He turned his gaze back to the starfield and shook his head in admiration. "Look, this is the most fantastic thing I've ever seen, but I don't see how it helps me."

The woman pointed. "Look there, there in the upper-right quadrant."

Stryker squinted up and saw for the first time something oval-shaped swinging down toward them. He shrugged. "So?"

"Look closer."

Stryker squinted harder. It was like tracking a high-thrown football in a night game, save that this football was golden in color, and tumbling rather than spiraling toward to him. "What the hell's that, some sort of satellite?"

"That, young man, is a caravanserai."

Intrigued, Stryker, still squinting, took a half step forward. "And what, exactly, is a caravanserai?"

"A caravanserai is an inn, in this case, an inn operated by The Brothers of All for the benefit of spacefarers in the Draguth System."

Stryker shook his head. "The Daguth System?"

"A binary system lying far beyond the Deneb Cluster. A system, as yet, undiscovered by Earth's astronomers."

Stryker winced. *Earth's astronomers? So, that's the con. She wants me to think she's an alien. Okay, I'll play along if it'll get me outta here.* He returned his gaze to the caravanserai. Closer now, it appeared more disk-shaped than oval, and, for the first time, he could see surface features, soaring towers, spiraling ramps, and yawning portals. Then something– something looking like a string of dirty golf balls held in line by a latticework of white tubular-scaffolding and propelled by three huge, outrigger-mounted engines–emerged from one of the portals. Stryker peered down at the woman, now visible only in profile. "And that, I suppose, is what this Altman dude thinks a starship will look like."

The woman gave vent to an amused laugh. "In his youth, Altman traveled on enough starships to know exactly what they look like.

Stryker shrugged. "If you say so. What is all this anyway, some sorta 3D projection?"

The woman's tone changed from amusement to exasperation. "No! It's not a projection, 3D or otherwise. It is a finely crafted work of alternate reality. In which, should you choose to enter, you will assume the persona of Quan Lin Jang, intergalactic soldier of fortune."

Stryker groaned and shot up a restraining hand. "Okay, let me get this straight. Your solution to my problem is to have me assume the role of a character in some sorta cyberspace opera?"

The woman sighed. "There's nothing 'cyber' about it. One lives and dies within an Altman composition, but not to worry, as you make the transition from this reality to that of Altman, you will be provided with all the knowledge, skills, and equipment needed to survive. As I see it, this is your best and only chance. You're a gambler, take it."

The sound of a car engine revving up jerked Stryker's attention back to the doorway behind him. Through it, he could see another of Big Minh's SUVs. This one was crouched facing the storefront. Beside the vehicle stood Big Minh himself, conferring with the driver, and gesturing toward the front of the shop. Crap! Looks like he's going to try and storm the building.

Stryker swung back to face the woman. "Okay, you've got a deal. What do I have to do?"

The woman gestured toward the starfield. "Start walking forward. You will be transitioned automatically."

Stryker took a deep breath and, hands stretched before him, started forward, expecting at any moment to feel the rough concrete of the shop's back wall against his fingertips.

It never happened.

#

One moment, he was shuffling across the uneven, starlit floor. The next, he was standing open-mouthed in the center of a sunny courtyard surrounded by lush greenery. From all around came the sound of water splashing and burbling in unseen fountains. Stryker shook his head in wonder. *It worked, it actually freaking worked.* It was only then, he noticed a gray-bearded man in a short, white tunic and sandals, standing amid the greenery, and beckoning to him. He shivered. *That's Altman, but how the hell do I know that?* As he started forward, there was a sound like cloth ripping, and the scene before him split vertically. The right side continued to display Altman and the garden while left showed Big Min's SUV crashing into the storefront, plowing thru the shop and coming to a halt against the back wall. Then darkness claimed him for the second time that evening.

When Stryker came to, things had changed yet again. Noise and movement swirled around him, and massive, ground-effect vehicles, piled high with oddly colored and even more oddly shaped objects, growled by on either side. While, far overhead, strings of, what looked like, yellow cargo containers snaked in and out of openings cut high into steel-gray walls of the hanger-like structure in which he now stood. He shook his head. *This is the caravanserai's central transit hub. How do I know that?*

Whoever designed the hanger did so without human comfort in mind. The overhead floodlights flickered in a manner likely to induce seizures, the air was thick with the smell of ozone and something like kerosene, and it was cold, so cold Stryker could see his breath puff out before him. He shivered, reached down to zip up his jacket, paused in mid-motion, and glanced down. He no longer wore his varsity jacket and slacks. Rather, he wore a gray, tight-fitting, one-piece garment, with dark-green shoulder patches. He grinned. *Son of a bitch! This is Quan Lin Jang's uniform.*

Close behind him, a horn bellowed.

He spun around to see one of the cargo carriers bearing down on him, yellow lights flashing, and its apelike driver bounding up and down in the cab and shaking a hairy fist. Stryker leaped aside, giving the driver the finger as he did so. The driver shot him an uncomprehending glance before returning to the task of piloting its massive vehicle. Ahead of the cargo carrier towered a forest of red gantry-cranes backed by a field of unblinking stars. Below the cranes, moored to the deck by unseen forces, floated dozens of starships identical to the one he had seen earlier. The cranes, unlike the ships, were in constant motion, loading them with the same sort of containers that moved overhead. One crane, however, worked at a slower pace unloading net after net of, what appeared to be, purple foliage from a battered-looking ship which, unlike the others, stood on the deck.

There was a distinct pop, and a shimmering, sprite-like creature, standing no more than six inches high, appeared on his left shoulder, and said, "Greetings, Stryker. I'm Mirket, Composition Expeditor. Something went wrong with your transition. I'll be your guide and mobile reference source until the problem's resolved."

Stryker shook his head. I can not catch a break. "Fine, Mirket, what do we do now?"

The sprite gestured toward another fast approaching cargo carrier. "Get out this traffic for a start." Then, motioning for Stryker to follow, Mirket flitted over to a pedway parallelling the route followed by the cargo haulers. Stryker pounded over to join the sprite. "Okay, where to now?"

Mirket made a follow-me-gesture saying, "To the Street of Shadows."

Stryker trotted after his new guide. "The Street of Shadows?"

"Yes, if your transition had gone properly, you would now be equipped with a boarding pass for the starship *Envy of Light* and be wearing a chameleon suit. The street is the only place I can get replacements on short notice."

Stryker frowned. "Okay, the boarding pass I think I get, but what's a chameleon suit, and why do I need it?"

"Quan Lin Jang's a wanted being, always on the run from someone or something, so he wears a chameleon suit when traveling. Dressed as you are, you might as well be standing under a hundred-meter high hologram flashing out the words: Attention all bounty hunters. Here stands Quan Lin Jang. Come get your money."

Stryker groaned. "There's a bounty on this guy?"

"Yes, unpaid gambling debts."

Stryker shook his head. Great. Out of the freaking frying pan and into gods only know what.

Mirket threw up a silence commanding hand muttering as it did so, "Oh, this is bad." The sprite hovered for a moment, eyes unfocused, as if accessing some distant data source, then said, "It appears that others transitioned at the same time as you. "

Stryker swore under his breath. Oh, crap! Big Minh's goons must have made it all the way to the back of the shop. He straightened up. "Is the old lady okay?"

Mirket made a calming gesture. "That 'old lady' is a member of an ancient and wily race of starfarers. She's quite safe. I assure you. It's you that we have to worry about."

Stryker gave his head a resigned shake. "Okay, then you better tell me more about this Quan Lin Jiang guy."

"Of course, Quan Lin Jang's a famous mercenary captain, a much-feared duelist, and an inveterate gambler."

Before Stryker could process all of this, a heavy-caliber pistol barked somewhere to their rear, and a bullet zinged overhead. He spun around to see a dozen or more overcoated figures racing toward him. That Big Minh's goons were still chasing him was, by now, no surprise, but Nicoli's presence amongst them came as a shock and a nasty one at that.

The Russian mobster bawled out, "You are dead, man, college boy."

Stryker raced for the cover of a passing cargo hauler as two more shots zipped by.

Behind him, someone, probably Big Minh, yelled, "Stop shooting, you Russian oaf. Kill him, and we'll never find those bonds."

Stryker drew the automatic from a shoulder holster he couldn't remember acquiring and crouched, waiting for the hauler to pass. As soon as it did, he emptied the clip at his pursuers, hitting none but forcing all of them to kiss the deck. He then spun around and raced after the sprite. Behind him came the screech and thud of multiple collisions and the howl of numerous alarms.

#

Stryker gazed yokel-like about him. Street of Shadows was an apt name. The lighting appeared set to approximate a fall evening on a planet with a sun weaker and redder than Earth's, and sepia-colored holograms of two-storied, half-timbered buildings fronted, what Mirket said were, single-story modular structures. The holograms changed at intervals as did their signage. The street itself teemed with all manner of odd-looking creatures: tall, green, mantis-like beings wearing desert-yellow capes, short, shuffling, quadrupeds looking like badgers, and gray, rubbery things resembling random lengths of garden hose, slithering amid the others, hissing warnings wherever they went.

Stryker turned to Mirket and, gesturing toward the milling crowd, said, "Who the heck are these guys?"

The sprite said, "Environmental refugees, for the most part, but there are also asteroid prospectors, tech traders and the like. The gray tubes are the result of a gene hacking experiment gone horribly wrong. They provide maintenance services on the ships mining gas giants." She then led Stryker to an otherwise unremarkable mid-block building with a sign over the door reading Incognito, which, as they approached, changed to read Best Aliases. Stryker stepped through the shop doorway into a low-ceilinged room with man-high cabinets lining the walls, but otherwise devoid of furniture. The proprietor– a tall, stooped humanoid with bushy eyebrows and four bulging, yellow eyes– beckoned him in. "Good evening, sir. How may we be of service?"

The sprite shot forward to hover between them. "I am the Composition Expeditor. My client requires a priority boarding pass for starship *Envy of Light*, a chameleon suit, a laser carbine, and a belt of energy clips."

The proprietor threw up its six-fingered hands in a placating gesture. "Endless apologies, Expeditor, I did not see you there. I will, of course, assist in any way I can, but, as you are aware, the law forbids trading in such items. And, even if some unscrupulous person were able to obtain them for your client, the price would be so great as to test the resources of the largest of the inner-world triads."

Mirket replied with some heat, "I don't have time for your silly games. This is a composition override. You will produce the items required and will produce them within the hour. I will pay all reasonable charges from my account."

The proprietor blanched. "Of course, Expeditor, but is this truly an override?"

"Yes, entities other than my client have gained access to the composition. At best, there will be instabilities and even circle traps. At worst, the composition may collapse in its entirety."

#

Less than an hour later, Stryker, now wearing a chameleon suit set to mimic the spacer-grays of starship crews, stepped out into the now dark street. He carried a laser carbine slung over his right shoulder and wore six box-like energy clips on his waist belt. The boarding pass, he carried in his vest-pocket. As they made their way back to the main transit hub, he turned to the sprite, saying, "Back there, you said something about circle traps. What are they?"

The sprite frowned. "They are damned if you do and damned if you don't sort of situations."

"Lovely, is there anything, in particular, that I should be on the lookout for?"

Mirket shrugged. "If the composition were running properly, you would have boarded *Envy of Light* by now, but now anything is possible. We could fall into a mini black hole or meet your double or even your triple around the next corner."

Stryker sighed. "Yeah, it's been that sort of day."

As they emerged from the Street of Shadows, a troop of green lizards scampered by. Each lizard stood half a head taller than Stryker and carried a variety of presumed weapons. He moved to fall in behind the fast-moving creatures, but Mirket hung back, looking shaken. Stryker swung back to face the sprite. "What's wrong now?"

Mirket gestured toward the fast departing lizards.

"Those are Hsia mercenaries."

"So?"

"They are from another Altman composition. They don't belong here."

"Well, they don't seem to mind my being here, and they're heading toward the central transit hub, so I'm going to follow them."

The Sprite, looking decidedly unhappy, flitted after him as he jogged off in pursuit of the long-striding Hsia.

#

When Stryker reached the part of the hanger deck where the starships were moored, he found half a dozen cargo haulers parked in a semicircle facing the foliage-hauling starship he saw earlier. For the first time, he noticed the words *Envy of Light* stenciled across the vessel's dinted bow. He nodded. That figures.

Movement elsewhere caught his eye. Between the semicircle of vehicles and the starship, towered a purple horror. The thing swayed cobra-like while spitting yellow foam from the tips of the dark-brown tentacles ringing the top of its swollen, tube-shaped body. Wherever the foam hit the hanger deck, small craters appeared, and an eye-stinging, greenish smoke billowed up. The creature gave off a smell like a back-alley garbage can at the end of a long summer weekend.

Stryker skidded to a halt and clasped a hand over his nose and mouth. "Phew! What the hell's that?"

Mirket, hovering behind him, peeked over his shoulder. "Oh, this keeps getting worse."

Stryker grimaced. "Don't tell me. This isn't in the composition either, right?"

The sprite made a despairing gesture. "None of this is in the composition."

The lizard soldiers drew themselves up in a two-deep line forming a barrier between the swaying, purple creature, and the *Envy of Light*.

Above the soldiers, a group of orange, crab-like creatures was gathered around, what looked like, a fire monitor protruding from an opening high up on the starship's side. One of the Hsia, an officer, judging by its numerous, scarlet-chevron tattoos, proceeded to engage in a heated exchange with the crabs.

Stryker glanced back at the sprite. "What's going on?"

"The starship's crew is demanding that the Hsia destroy the Anemone."

"The Anemone's the purple thing, right?"

"Yes. They are an invasive species. *The Envy of Light* must have unknowingly brought this one here hidden amid the cargo of purple foliage she carried. Anemones are slow-moving, but they grow and multiply quickly, and are destructive of starships, their cargos, and crews."

Stryker glanced over at the double line of lizard soldiers. "So why aren't these guys doing something about it?"

"The Brothers of All, regard all life as sacred. They must have ordered the Hsia to protect the Anemone from the wrath of the starship crew."

Stryker gestured upward toward the crabs. "And what's the crew threatening to do?"

The Sprite shrugged. "As I've already said, none of this is supposed to be happening, but it appears that the crew is threatening to spray the docks with DNA dispersant."

Stryker took an involuntary step backward. "And that would be a bad thing, right?"

The sprite nodded. "For all the unprotected life forms assembled here, yes."

"And what's the head lizard saying about it all?"

"The Hsia commander is saying that it has orders to use force, if necessary, to protect the Anemone from harm."

Stryker nodded. "This is one of your circle traps, isn't it?"

"I fear so, yes."

The shouting match between the starship crew and the Hsia appeared to be over for the moment. So, Stryker took the opportunity to study the Anemone more closely. The creature was rocking back and forth on stubby protuberances that served for legs and squirting more corrosive foam onto the deck. Stryker noticed, for the first time, a series of vertical seams running the length of the Anemone's body. He glanced over at the sprite, still hovering beside him. "How do these things reproduce?"

Mirket frowned. "Mitosis, most likely."

"And this one looks about ready to split into what, six or eight new individuals?"

"More like ten, I should think."

Stryker felt a surge of irritation. The caravanserai could be destroyed, and these clowns were doing nothing. He paused. So, why do I care? Oh, crap! That's Quan Lin Jang's thinking. He's now part of me, or I'm part of him or whatever. Either way, I've got to act. He squared his shoulders, took a deep breath, and strode over to the Hsia officer.

The lizard commander threw up a forestalling three-fingered hand. "Stay back, spacer, lest those crazy crabs make good their threats."

Stryker gestured toward the Anemone. "I've seen the damage these creatures can inflict on starships. This one's on the verge of replicating itself. You must get rid of it before it does so."

The Hsia officer managed a human-like shake of its head. "Understood, but my orders are to protect the Anemone from harm."

At this, the crew of the *Envy of Light* gave vent to a series of unmistakably rude noises. The Hsia troopers responded with raised weapons and a chorus of angry hisses.

Stryker held up his hands in a calming gesture. "What if we can rid the caravanserai of the Anemone without harming the creature?"

The Hsia officer flicked out a black tongue. "That is much to be desired, but can it be done?"

"With your help, yes."

Mirket tugged at Stryker's sleeve. "Whatever you have in mind, you better be quick about it. Those pursuing you can't be far behind."

Stryker glanced back. "Can you locate them for me?"

The sprite nodded and stared off into the distance, consulting her database. Moments later, she said, "They've been searching the Street of Shadows, and are now headed this way."

Stryker swung back to the Hsia officer and gestured upward. "Can you contact the operators of the gantry crane that's been unloading that purple crap?"

"Yes, of course, but to what end?"

"We need to herd the Anemone under the crane so that the operator can drop a cargo net over it. Okay?"

The Hisa commander nodded, hissed an order to one of its soldiers, a scarred veteran with a flaming grenade tattooed on its right cheek. The officer then hissed further orders into a triangular device strapped to the back of its hand.

Meanwhile, the veteran doubled over to the nearest cargo hauler and hissed orders up to the driver, who took offense, bounding up and down and shrieking. The veteran responded by hoisting a lethal-looking, tube-shaped device to its shoulder.

The driver immediately ceased its bounding and shrieking, and, with many a venomous glance at the veteran, began inching its vehicle toward the Anemone, herding the foam-spitting creature back toward the base of the gantry crane.

The Hsia officer reached down and tapped Stryker on the shoulder. "What are we to do with the Anemone once we have it netted?"

"Dump it in the biggest, strongest cargo container you can find; one that can withstand the effects of that foam, and yet keep it alive until the crabs can drop it off someplace, an uninhabited asteroid, perhaps, where it can do no harm."

The Hsia officer bobbed its head in eager agreement. "One of the bulk containers used by the Outer Mark Line should suffice."

The Mirket tugged at Stryker's sleeve, and he turned to see a mob of blue-gray overcoats less than a football field length away and surging toward them. "You better find yourself some cover," he said, jerking his thumb back toward the crescent of parked cargo haulers.

The sprite shook her head. "No, as Composition Expediter, my place is at your shoulder."

A shot cracked past Stryker's ear, and he threw himself to the deck, taking Mirket with him. He then rolled, unslung the laser carbine, and slapped an energy clip in place. Big Min's thugs continued shooting, and a lizard soldier screamed and flopped down beside Stryker, yellow fluid spurting from the gaping hole torn in its chest. At the same moment, Nikolai bellowed, "Big Min's dead. You won't get away this time, Stryker."

He glanced up. Nikolai was less than thirty yards away, aiming an ugly-looking, black pistol at him. The gun cracked twice, but both shots went wide.

Stryker's new persona asserted itself. He sighted down the barrel of the carbine and squeezed the firing stud. A pencil-thin bolt of blue light flashed from the muzzle punching a hole through one of Nikolai's legs, dropping him to the foam-cratered decking. The smell of burnt flesh wafted back over Stryker, making him gag. Meanwhile, another hood raced forward, working the pump-action of his weapon, blasting off shot after shot. Stryker froze. Sonofabitch, even Ferret Face, made the transition. Then Quan Lin Jang's combat reflexes cut in, and he rolled to his right, seconds before a shotgun blast struck the decking where he had been lying. With bullets ricocheting off the deck all around him, he shot Ferret Face in the forehead and, a moment later, brought down the charging Bullet Head with two quick shots to the chest.

The Hsia, with the flaming grenade tattoo, landed beside him, gave Stryker an approving slap on the shoulder, and brought its weapon into action. The tube-shaped weapon threw out the ear-punishing whine of a jet engine and gave off a stink worse than burning rubber, but it cut down the thugs still standing in a single sweep of retina-searing, blue light.

A moment later, something nudged Stryker's shoulder. He rolled onto his back and squinted up to see the Hsia commander standing over him. The officer's mouth moved, but Stryker could hear nothing for the ringing in his ears.

Mirket perched on Stryker's shoulder and yelled, "The Hsia commander says that while it fully understands and approves of your actions, you now must leave. If you don't, the Brothers of All will order you arrested and charged with the killing of sentient beings."

"What?" Stryker said, cupping his still ringing ear.

The sprite hovered closer, yelling even louder, "It`s another circle trap, but this time it's working in your favor, but you must board the *Envy of Light* now. You can stay here no longer."

Stryker glanced up. The crabs were lowering a boarding tube down from high up on the side of the *Envy of Light*. While to his right, the operators of the gantry crane were loading the netted Anomie, still writhing and spitting into a slate-gray container with alien-looking symbols stenciled the length of its battered side.

He staggered to his feet and stumbled toward the boarding tube. The Hsia, with the flaming grenade tattoo, fell in beside him. Stryker turned to Mirket and said, "Tell the Hsia commander I'll go quietly. I don't need an escort."

The sprite yelled back, "This soldier isn`t escorting you. It, too, is being expelled from the caravanserai for killing sentient beings."

As Stryker entered the boarding tube, he saw Mirket still perched on his shoulder. "You're coming, too?"

The sprite nodded and yelled back, "Yes. I wish to see how this version of the composition ends."

Vincent Morgan lives in the fishing port of Steveston, British Columbia, is an avid reader of science fiction with a particular fondness for space opera, has completed the Science Fiction Writers Master Course with Gotham Writers Workshop and several courses with LitReactor. His short story, *To Allegiance Recalled,* was awarded Silver Honorable Mention by Writers of the Future. And his work appears in several anthologies, including Explorers Beyond The Horizon, First Contact Imminent, and Aliens Among Us.

A RIPPLE IN SPACE
BY OWEN MORGAN

Hyperion System, Earth Cruiser Paris, October 31, 2145

Subcommander Alex Whistler rapped on the captain's door. While he waited, he brought up a 3D projection of his orders on his wrist tattoo. Before he could summon a new image, the door opened without a sound. He stepped inside a dark-paneled room and stood to attention. From behind a fine polished, oak desk, Captain Bremen, a thin man with a frost of white hair adorning his head, held a red and white banned glue tube and squeezed a tiny bead of glue onto the base of a radar array and affixed it behind the bridge of a model ship.

The captain's eyes flicked up. "Ah, good to finally meet you. It's Subcommander, Alex Whistler, right?"

"Yes, captain. I transferred over from the Nelson two hours ago. I would have reported sooner, but I was told you were unavailable."

Bremen pointed to a plush, leather chair. "Take a seat. Don't worry about that. Rank has its privileges. I, for one, like to build models, as you can see. But enough about my hobbies. What's your take on the Xion negotiations?"

"It's as delicate as your model, sir. The native population of Xion—."

The captain made a dismissive gesture. "Bah, I don't care one whit about the native population, and neither do the politicians back home. You were assigned here because of your first contact with the Sun Lords. I need to know if they'll fight us over Xion. That piece of rock is a jump-off point into three star systems."

Alex cleared his throat. "They'll fight us. The Sun Lords, as their name implies they believe they have a divine right over all worlds orbiting suns."

"I see." He clipped away another plastic piece from the molding and cleaned the edge with a knife. "Perhaps I was a bit hasty a moment ago, Who do you think the natives will ally with the Sun Lords or us?"

"Unknown, sir. Despite what we believed back in the twentieth century, not all worlds are politically united. Some of the nations will side with us. I suppose it comes down to our ambassador and which nations she sways toward Earth."

He nodded. "Sounds like the native tribes in the Seven Years War. Some sided with France and others with Britain. I have read a descriptive term for the Xion. Apparently, another race once shared their world. Have you heard anything along these lines?"

"A xenological survey found books in a forgotten city on the southern continent. The people from this continent called the Xion shapeless."

"Yes, I remember in the report, the linguists were arguing over the meaning of Xion, but I'm a fighting man, and I'll leave those matters to the academics."

"I agree, sir. Space is no place for academic debate."

"There is one more thing, subcommander. I understand your first contact with the Sun Lords involved an unusual ship."

Alex raised a thin eyebrow. "Sir, I don't know if I can talk about that."

"Look, if we're going to get into a fight with them, I want to know all their capabilities. Don't worry. I have some contacts inside naval intelligence. You won't be telling me anything I shouldn't know."

"That was two years ago. I was a junior officer at the time. We're out on patrol in the Isis sector, and one of our SOSUS buoys detected something, although the contact only showed up for a second. The captain brought the ship in to investigate. Next thing anyone knew, a pair of torpedoes appeared on our screens, racing toward our starboard side. Our close range defense autocannon destroyed one, but the second hit us midships, tore an eighty-foot hole in the hull."

The captain put down his glue and tapped a finger on the desk. "Thanks, that does answer a few concerns I had on that situation. It sounds like they have some sort of cloaking device."

"It would seem that the enemy can mask themselves until their ships are almost on top of our vessels. Is there anything else, sir?"

"No, go to the bridge and get settled."

As Alex stepped through the doorway, he called after him. "Your brother was on your ship?"

"Yes, sir."

"The thought of getting back at those bastards for killing him ever cross your mind?"

"I would be lying if I said no."

"Good. Let that motivate you. I need you to work on some theories as to how the enemy can avoid detection. It has been a year, no doubt the Sun Lords have produced more of these ships."

#

Alex entered the bridge via a turbo elevator and sat at his computer console. He keyed in his password and pressed his thumb against the DNA scanning pad. After familiarizing himself with the bridge crews' credentials, he typed a laborious twenty-four digit naval intelligence code. The computer searched for a moment then flashed the words: No new data found.

"Captain on deck," the bridge officer announced.

Bremen took his command chair and punched up information from the console on the armrest. He looked to the communications officer who pressed a button and nodded. "Attention, this is Captain Bremen. As of 20:00 talks with the Sun Lords have broken down. Our ambassador has withdrawn, and we'll rendezvous with her in the next three hours. Our job is to escort the ambassador and her staff to Cairo Station. At this point, the enemy has made no aggressive moves against us, but hostilities could break out at any time."

Bremen walked over to Alex's station. "I guess its too much to hope you've come up with anything on these invisible ships?"

Alex called up a schematic of the 'Battle of Talos.' He pointed to different parts of the map. "As you can see, the enemy torpedoes appeared after we detected an anomaly over at this point. I had a thought after watching you building your ship. Was that model of a British World War Two corvette, one of those sub chasers?"

"Yes, but how does that help us detect them?"

"Have you read about folding space?"

"Yes, the theory of hiding objects in a pocket in space. But no one has managed to fold space."

"Begging your pardon, sir, but no one from Earth has achieved folding. I think the Sun Lords might have done it."

"You mean we'll act like a corvette, and the enemy will act like a submarine?"

"Precisely. I may have found a solution, and we can make use of the Athens. She's close by."

"And how is a science ship going to help us?"

"Her instruments are calibrated for detecting dust particles, and other materials the Navy doesn't consider important. In theory, the folding of space will leave distortions like a rock skipping over water. In other words, she'll leave a trail."

#

Bremen brought the ship into orbit around the Gas Giant Odin. Alex frowned as he looked at his screen. "No sign of the ambassador's ship. She's not as fast as us, but she was closer."

"I can see that, switch to long-range. I want to see if they're hiding somewhere in the system."

"Nothing on the scope. Perhaps they're laying low until we arrive."

"All right, she could be running dark. Send out a pair of fighters and scout the inner system. They'll also provide an early warning if the enemy got here before us."

Two Long Lance fighters rocketed from the port bay, skirting an asteroid field and disappearing around the gas giant. Long-range sensors kept track of the fighters, which appeared as red triangles designated C 1 and C 2. The fighters disappeared from the screen a few seconds later. Bremen let out a long breath and steepled his fingers. The fighter images reappeared half a minute later.

One of the pilots called in, "Captain, we can't see anything but miles of stars. Do you want us to swing around Thor's Hammer? I know she's just a little iceball, but you never know."

"Affirmative. Swing around, but go to maximum thrust. I don't want the two of you caught out there all alone."

The two fighters veered away from Odin and swung around Thor's Hammer. C 2 began to fall behind C 1 as radio chatter crackled between the two craft. Bremen pressed the communication button. "C 2, you're falling behind. What's the problem?"

The distorted pilot's voice crackled back, "Sorry, sir. I've hit some interference. Maybe its from the sun. I can't be sure."

Another contact appeared on screen. One of the bridge crew called out, "It's the ambassador's ship, and she's coming in fast."

"Great," Bremen grunted. "Helm, move us toward the ambassador's ship and close the distance with our fighters."

Alex turned to Bremen. "Sir, remember our thoughts on the enemy leaving a trail? What if the fighter crossed the path of one of their stealth ships?"

"Christ, launch the first alert fighters, get the rest of the wing on standby."

Two more fighters lurched from the starboard launch bay, hurtling toward the ambassador's ship at top speed while C 2 continued to lag behind its wingman. Another blip appeared on the main screen. An inbound torpedo was targeting the ambassador's ship. C 1 dropped sound decoys in the hope of distracting the torpedoes' sensors. The fighter swung about hard, flying a counter course toward the torpedoes point of origin and firing his twin railguns. The hypervelocity rounds struck nothing but a small rogue asteroid, fragmenting the rock. The torpedo changed course and chased after the zig-zagging decoy.

"Close the distance and bring torpedo tubes alpha through delta online. Load all tubes and wait for my command," Bremen ordered.

The proximity alert screamed, and a second torpedo appeared on the screen. Bremen's eyes narrowed. "Tell those flyboys to take care of that one. We've got our hands full."

The ambassador's ship fired up her engines, moving toward the Paris. The torpedo fell away from the decoy, circling. Alex banged his fists on his console. "What in the name of Fraya is that idiot doing? If that torpedo reacquires them."

The targeting computer denoted the optimal firing distance at over three thousand meters while the main screen was ablaze with torpedoes and fighters. The first torpedo turned one-hundred and eighty degrees, moving straight toward the ambassador's ship. Alex kept an eye on the closing distance. "Captain, there's no way we will intercept the torpedo in time."

Bremen sat on the edge of his seat like a great cat about to pounce. His finger lingering over the firing button. When the firing range counted down to three thousand meters, he tapped the button, and three torpedoes lanced into space.

The first torpedo exploded behind the target, the shockwave knocking it twenty degrees off course. The enemy torpedo changed course and reacquired the ship. The last two remaining torpedoes from the Paris closed, but both detonated before striking their target.

Bremen frowned. "What the hell happened?"

"Enemy torpedo deployed countermeasures, sir. The torpedo will hit the ambassador's ship in forty seconds," Alex said.

Bremen thumped his fist on the armrest. "Options?"

"Nothing we can do. Wait, captain, it's C 2."

All eyes fixed on the main screen. C 2 positioned itself between the torpedo and the ship, then winked out of existence replaced by an expanding debris field that spread across the quadrant.

Bremen smoothed his hand over his hair. "Alex, do we know the approximate range of the enemy's torpedoes?"

"Yes, sir. The enemy has a range of about three thousand four hundred meters, assuming they have not increased the range in the last year."

Bremen tapped the communication button. "All squadron leaders redeploy to sector eight and fire tactical nukes along a thirty-degree arc. Helm move us beside the ambassador's ship and prepare to receive the ambassador shuttle forthwith."

Alex watched the screen as the Paris' fighters launched a barrage of nuclear-tipped missiles in a fan-like formation, each one detonating several kilometers apart. The computer registered each explosion and resulting fallout and debris.

A shuttle departed from the ambassador's ship and landed on the port side bay. Bremen smiled. "Those nukes should have taken care of the bastard. Alex, follow me."

Down in the landing bay, Ambassador Ashanti stood with her arms folded across her chest, eyes cast to the floor. Bremen marched over to her and introduced himself. "Welcome aboard, Ambassador.

This is Subcommander Alex Whistler. He has some experience with the enemy. Perhaps you can help to fill us in on their intentions."

"Thank you, captain. But they're not the enemy. The Sun Lords and Earth had almost reached an agreement."

"Pardon me ambassador, but the Sun Lords just tried to stick a torpedo up your ship's aft section. I would say that qualifies as the actions of an enemy."

She frowned. "I am not some stupid diplomat who doesn't understand when hostilities have broken out. I mean, the Xion started the war between Earth and the Sun Lords."

"What are you talking about? The Xion have roughly Earth equivalent twenty-first-century tech. They'd be lucky to get a shuttle into orbit, let alone attack one of our ships."

Alex tried to speak, but a blaring claxon cut him off. A computerized voice called out, "Proximity alert, brace for impact."

The hanger bay heaved, and tungsten reinforced bulkheads swelled and buckled. The impact pitched people across the hanger, sending them crashing into aircraft, machinery, weapons, and walls as lights flickered and surrendered to darkness.

Alex sprawled between two plastic containers. He tasted copper and ran his tongue over his teeth, checking for breaks. Spitting and coughing, he groped in the darkness and used the containers to stand. "Captain, are you there?"

Bremen called back, "I'm here. Find the ambassador and see if she's injured."

Alex fumbled around splintered and sharp-edged boxes and crates, stumbling over debris, calling for the ambassador. The emergency lights flashed to life, bathing Ashanti's still body, crumpled between the bulkhead and an autoloader machine. He reached down and pressed his fingers against her neck, no pulse.

"Captain, she's gone."

Bremen cursed and waved him over. "Let's get back to the bridge."

Red emergency lighting bathed the bridge as the crew worked to ascertain damage and casualties. Bremen looked over a sailor's shoulder at the information flowing across the screen. He shook his head, balling his hands into fists. He addressed the crew through the ship-wide communications array. "This is the captain. We've sustained significant damage. The enemy chose to use a conventional warhead, and we've no idea if the enemy has any remaining nuclear warheads in their arsenal. Also, while our long-range sensors were knocked out during the battle, our fighters might have driven the enemy ship off. We'll retrieve our fighter squadrons and effect repairs while we wait for the Athens to rendezvous with us."

Bremen patted Alex on the shoulder. "Any idea of what the Xion might have done for her to call them the enemy and not the Sun Lords?"

He shook his head. "I would only be guessing. The Xion may have sabotaged the negotiations. Perhaps they realized the talks would only result in the partition of their world. Also, for all, we know the Xion might have infiltrated the Sun Lord's High Command and are sending their ships against us."

#

The Athens dropped into system four hours after the battle and sent a shuttle over to the Paris. Bremen and Alex greeted Captain Katrina Parshikov in the starboard bay. She extended a delicate hand to each. "Pleased to meet both of you. I should tell you the damage is quite extensive on the other side of your ship."

Bremen nodded. "We know, captain. The subcommander and I were on the port side when the Sun Lords hit us."

"I understand talks broke down with the Sun Lords. Do you know if the ambassador has withdrawn?"

"She's dead. We were all in the other hanger when the enemy hit us with a torpedo."

"Tell me, is there anything thing we can do to assist?"

Alex gestured toward a screen on the wall. He called up a replay of the battle. "As you can see, the enemy doesn't register on the screen until they have fired their torpedoes. Your ship has more finely honed instruments. Perhaps you can detect their presence?"

She frowned. "We could try and augment your detection devices. I don't think having a science vessel in a combat zone would be very helpful."

"Agreed." Bremen jabbed a thumb at the screen. "Ma'am, I have no idea when they'll attack again. We need your people and equipment over here, pronto."

Bremen's wrist tattoo chimed, he answered in a gruff tone. "This had better be important."

A woman's voice replied. "Captain, this is Doctor Williams. The ambassador's body is gone. I sent down two orderlies to retrieve her body, and they found nothing."

Alex's eyes narrowed. "Captain, remember the meaning of the name, Xion?"

"What? Oh, yes, the Xion are called shapeless. What of it?"

"We've heard about shapeshifters, what if the Xion can change form?"

"I'll need to get back to you, doctor." He tapped his wrist. "Sergeant Tanaka gather a squad. The ambassador's body is missing, and we have reason to believe she is a shapeshifter. Secure all of the ship's critical sections. Report back to me when you have found her."

Alex punched in a code on an arm's locker and handed a rifle to Bremen and took one for himself. "Captain, I think we should leave Ms. Parshikov to her work."

"Agreed. Let's meet up with some of the marines and find out what the hell is going on aboard my ship."

As Alex and Bremen sprinted down a corridor leading to one of the ship's magazines, the captain's wrist communicator sounded. "What's happened?"

"Captain, the ambassador's ship is experiencing engine trouble. Her captain reports a dangerous energy spike."

"Can they solve the problem?"

"The captain doesn't sound confident. In fact, he wants to send another shuttle over with essential personnel. He says if the energy continues to spike, the ship might explode."

"Sir, this might be a trick," Alex said.

"How could this be a trick?"

"We might have a saboteur on board. What if there are more aboard the ambassador's ship who plan to come over and do the same to the Paris?"

Angry voices echoed from farther down the hallway. Alex led Bremen to the magazine, where three marines armed with M-90 assault rifles kept a close watch on anyone entering the area.

"What's the problem?" Bremen demanded.

All three stood to attention. A corporal stepped forward. "Begging your pardon, sir, we've heard a marine was found dead one floor below."

"Has anyone confirmed the marine is dead?"

"No, sir. But we're down a man. There should be four to guard the magazine."

A burst of automatic fire ripped through the assembled men. One marine slumped over as fragments of his skull showered the wall. A second man was spun around by the force of a round striking him. Alex reached out and grasped Bremen's shoulder and pulled him back into the corridor. The last marine turned and fired at the unseen attacker. Muzzle flashes lit the hall as golden cartridges littered the floor. He stopped and flipped a clip into his rifle, but a hail of bullets tore through his body, punching into kevlar armor, bone and flesh. He dropped to the floor, coughing and spitting up blood.

From out of sight, the sound of feet striking metal floorplates faded away. Alex pressed himself against the floor and pointed his rifle toward the gore-smeared wall beside the magazine door. The injured marine lumbered forward, favoring his left arm.

Bremen pulled him into the corridor. "Son, did you see who shot you?"

"No. I just felt the round smash into my shoulder. I think the kevlar absorbed most of the impact."

"Captain," Alex motioned with his rifle back down the hallway. "Your place is on the bridge. We'll take care of whoever is out there."

"You're right. I was damn stupid, leaving the bridge in the first place. But I want whoever is shooting at us dead before I go back." He turned to the marine. "What's your name?"

"Rodriguez, sir."

"All right, Rodriguez, we're going to find the bastard who shot you."

Alex crawled on his hands and knees up to the corridor. He took in a deep breath and peered around the corner. Only the bodies of the marines, blood, and spent cartridges greeted him. He stood and stepped over the fallen men with Bremen and Rodriguez, who retrieved his rifle, in tow. The metal stair plates banged as they descended to the next level.

Alex noticed a closed-door and signaled Rodriguez to cover him. He placed his palm on the identification pad next to the door. The door opened with a faint click. He pushed on the door with one hand until it swung into the room.

A shadow moved at the edge of his vision. A man, dressed in orderly's fatigues, darted up from behind a pile of plastic crates, arms raised above his head. "Don't shoot."

"What are you doing down here?" Alex demanded, keeping his weapon trained on the man.

"I was sent here to get more medical supplies. Then I heard the shooting. I closed the door and hoped whoever was shooting wouldn't find me."

Bremen called into the room. "That's fine. But you're staying in this room until we find the shooter."

Alex closed the door, and Bremen entered a security code to lock it. Rodriguez took point as they advanced down a passageway bathed in an eerie crimson light. Alex brought up the rear, glancing backward every thirty seconds. Rodriguez pointed his rifle around the corner and checked the video display attached to the top of his weapon. "Captain, I can see a closed door at the end of the passage."

Before Bremen could reply, his communicator chimed. "Captain, the ambassador's second shuttle will dock with us in three minutes. Do you have any further instructions?"

"Yes, begin moving us away from the ambassador's ship. Try and keep that shuttle from docking for ten minutes. I'll be back on the bridge soon, and get some marines down to the magazine ASAP."

Bremen motioned toward the door. "All right, marine, lead the way."

When Rodriguez reached the door, he nudged it with his barrel and stepped through into a four-way intersection. Alex crouched behind him and squinted ahead into the darkness beyond. "Somethings wrong. The emergency lights should be illuminating the hallway."

Bremen nodded. "You're right. We're going down the starboard side. Maybe the lights still work in that section."

Rodriguez sprinted and turned right into the intersection. A burst of automatic fire peppered the wall, and one bullet ricocheted off his helmet. He stumbled back and slid down the wall, his breathing short and sharp.

As the rifle fire died away, a man called out, "You there, throw down your weapons and come out with your hands up."

Bremen dropped his rifle and marched around the corner where six marines confronted him. "Put down your weapons, you idiots."

The marines lowered their weapons. One of them stepped forward. "Sorry, sir. We've been fighting an unknown number of enemies, and most of the emergency lights are shot out down here."

"Do you boys need to go back for retraining? Get your night fighting vision gear and find this enemy and kill it."

Alex motioned for Rodriguez to follow. Bremen crossed his arms and shook his head. "Are you all right, son?"

He nodded and grinned. "Yes. But I'm getting tired of being shot."

Bremen tapped his wrist tattoo. "Sergeant Tanaka, have you found the ambassador?"

"No, sir. I've had to station marines throughout the ship. We don't have enough men to both guard and search."

"Forget the ambassador. I think the shooter is now in the guise of a marine."

"Captain, I've lost three marines so far, which one am I looking for?"

"Just one. What does the marine found a deck below the magazine look like?"

"She's a tall redhead. Private, Pearl Anderson."

"That's no longer Anderson. Tell your men to try and capture, but be prepared to kill her."

A burst of automatic fired cut off the conversation. Alex led the charge along the hallway. He turned the corner, and his boot hit something slick, and he fell forward, crashing into a wall.

Rodriguez stepped around him, rifle held against his shoulder. "God in Heaven," he muttered. Alex stumbled to his feet and found himself surrounded by blood and gore from four marines.

Bremen pointed at a trail of bloody footprints. "I'll wager a week's shore leave on Vegas II, that's our shooter's trail."

Alex took point, following each diminishing footprint as the blood wore off the boots. He crouched beside a hallway and held his rifle around the corner, as Rodriguez did earlier. His screen showed a marine trying to access a palm scanner controlled door. Bremen mouthed the words. "Kill it."

Rodriguez stood and fired while Alex and Bremen knelt before him, unleashing a torrent of fire. The redheaded marine shook from each impact, her body rippling. Alex switched to automatic fire and emptied his clip into her. She fell backward under the surging fire, dropping her rifle, which discharged several times. Rodriguez crumpled, knocking Alex to the floor. As Bremen pulled Rodriguez away, the marine's head slipped to the side, a bloody hole torn through his neck.

Bremen swore. "Alex, make sure that thing doesn't get up again."

Alex found a grayish octopus-like being, its torso perforated and oozing a clear, viscous liquid from each wound. He kicked away the rifle and waited for the captain who strode over, aimed his rifle at the creature and fired until he ran out of ammunition.

"Come on, Alex. Let's get back to the bridge."

#

The screen displayed the second shuttle moving toward the Paris. Bremen sat, with a grunt, in his command chair and tapped the communication button. "Captain Parshikov, I want this channel secured before we continue."

"OK, Captain, we're able to speak. What news do you have for me?"

"The Xion are shapeshifters. Their true form is like an octopus. We lost several marines trying to stop one of their agents."

"That's incredible, a polymorphic race. That explains why the talks broke down. The Xion assumed human form and set us against the Sun Lords."

"How are your people faring with augmentations to my communications array?"

"Sorry, Captain, but the military technology is not as compatible with civilian tech as I hoped. We'll need several days, and for all I know, a space station to facilitate the required changes."

"I don't think the enemy will afford us the time or a space station. I'm afraid we will need your ship's presence in a combat zone."

She remained silent for a moment. "I understand."

"Very well. I will contact you later with my battle plan."

He signed off and turned his attention to the main screen. The shuttle aligned with the Paris and waited as the two vessels established a seal. The hanger bays were too damaged for a ship of that size to attempt a landing, and first alert fighters took priority over civilians.

"Captain," one of the bridge crew said. "The ambassador's ship has fired up her engines, and she's moving toward us."

"What? How far away is she now?"

"Four kilometers."

"Hail them."

"No response."

"Are the people all aboard from the shuttle?"

"Almost, sir. But they need more time to bring equipment onboard."

Alex called over his shoulder, "Captain, we have to assume the worst about who is in charge of the ship."

Bremen slammed his fist on the armrest. "Helm, move us away, keep our distance, and bring torpedo tube alpha online.

The ambassador's ship continued to accelerate, closing the distance with each passing second. Bremen's brow furrowed. "Hail them again."

"Nothing, sir. I'm not even sure they are listening."

"Fire torpedo one."

A torpedo jumped from the aft launcher and streaked toward the target. The ambassador's ship went to full burn. When the ship closed within two thousand meters, it detonated. A few seconds later, the bridge went dark as a shock wave assaulted the Paris. Alex held on reflexively to his console, but his harness held him in place.

"Damage," Bremen called from the darkness.

One of the bridge crew replied. "Impossible to tell. Some of our computers are down for the moment."

Bremen removed his harness and strode through the darkness and leaned over Alex's shoulder. "How are our short-range sensors?"

"All good. The only ship near us is the Athens."

"The only ship we can detect," he grumbled. "Is she damaged?"

"No, they were too far away from the blast."

"Fine. Assuming we still have engines, move us close to the ship and tell them to expect casualties."

#

Alex and the rest of the crew cheered as the regular lighting flickered to life, replacing the emergency lights. Bremen beckoned him to the overhead screen. "As you can see, I've positioned the Athens to our stern. She'll act as a radar-picket ship in the same way American destroyers did the same for the Allies in the final days of World War Two against the kamikazes. I hope her captain has not oversold their abilities to detect the enemy."

"Doubtful, the Athens would go down with us."

"I just got the damage report. The blast damaged a lot of electronics, but we can move and fight. The Athens should be able to detect hundreds of substances, both natural and artificial."

"Sounds good. But won't the Sun Lord's ship target the Athens and then fight us while we're blind?"

"I thought of that. We're going to mimic as an escort. If she were in front, then I would worry about your idea. I'm hoping the range of her sensors gives us time to destroy their ship."

Bremen ordered a course toward Cairo Station. Four of the ship's five engines flared to life, allowing the Athens to maintained a following distance of five hundred meters, keeping in the Paris' shadow. Bremen also ordered a circuitous route around the gas giant known as Odin's Eye in hopes of catching the enemy's attention.

Alex poured over the information sent over from the Athens, hoping to find some way of penetrating the enemy's cloak. But despite several hours of reading, if there was a solution, it alluded him.

"Incoming message from the Athens," said the communication's officer.

Bremen nodded. Katrina appeared on the main screen. "We've detected a strong radiation signature in quadrant seventeen by nine. It could be one of their nuclear-tipped torpedoes."

"Thank you, captain. From now on, send all messages via encryption."

The Paris moved toward the coordinates with the Athens following her course.

Alex cleared his throat. "Captain, is it time to launch the first alert fighters? But remember, we can only launch two fighters at the same time."

"Negative, we'll wait and see if the radiation is natural or one of their weapons."

"Understood. We're within weapons range of anything inside the quadrant."

"Action stations. Bring all torpedo tubes online, load missiles."

An encrypted message arrived at Bremen's console. He decrypted the message which read: radiation signature increasing but remaining stationary.

"Do we remain on course?" Alex said.

"Yes, continue until we can gain a visual identification. The moment we are close enough, I want whatever is giving off the radiation on the main screen."

A minute later, the main screen switched from a tactical view to a sea of stars set against a black palette. Alex increased magnification by two-hundred percent. In the middle of the screen sat a triangular object. Before he could increase the magnification to determine the object's true purpose, the screen flicked back to tactical with two torpedoes inbound, one for each ship. Point defense cannons with spinning barrels unleashed a flood of firepower, the torpedoes weaving around the hail of tungsten rounds. One of the torpedoes ignited into a fireball as the shells found their mark.

"Launch first alert fighters. And tell the hanger crews their lives depend on the speed with which they can launch those fighters."

Another encrypted message: Two more decoys detected. Recommend using fighters to destroy them. We're in the process of detecting the enemy's trail, will advise.

The second torpedo exploded meters before the hull as a fighter nipped in between and fired its railguns. Alex turned to Bremen. "Sir, advise we fire a broadside in the general area of the incoming torpedoes. We might get lucky."

"Agreed. Set all warheads to explode at different ranges. I want to blanket the area."

The Paris turned toward the original torpedo path and fired all railguns and unleashed a full spread of torpedoes and salvo of missiles. The mass of ordinance hurled through the void, moments later, a series of detonations registered on screen. Bremen ordered the ship toward the explosions hoping to present a smaller profile while the last of the fighters launched and formed a protective phalanx around the ship.

Another torpedo contact flashed on the screen, surrounded by a cloud of dots, each one some form of countermeasure. The fighters fired their railguns, but the cloud moved to intercept each kinetic strike. The torpedo veered between a pair of fighters and moved at high speed toward the Athens.

Bremen tapped the communication button. "Katrina, get your people to the escape pods, I don't think we can intercept the torpedo."

Dozens of escape pods fired out from the Athens as the torpedo struck the bridge, and the ship ignited. Serrated, hot steel, tungsten, and melting plastic erupted and tumbled through space.

The bridge crew fell silent as the wreckage stretched across their screens. Alex wiped a hand across his sweaty forehead. "Captain, we received an encrypted message just before the torpedo hit the Athens."

"Don't keep me in suspense. Decrypt the message."

"It's a software upgrade. We can track any trail left behind by their torpedos."

"Oustanding. Have our fighters formed into attack formation and stand by for orders. Move us closer to the wreckage of the Athens. I want the enemy to think we're picking up survivors."

The Paris circled the debris of the Athens and opened her port side landing bay to the life pods. Bremen watched the clock. "Ten minutes, what the hell are the Sun Lord's waiting for an invitation?"

"Captain, our fighters are getting low on fuel. One of the squadrons is requesting permission to land at the starboard bay." Alex said.

"Permission granted. But stagger the landings, no more than two at a time. I want to maintain the illusion of going through the motions."

Four fighters landed before an enemy torpedo registered on screen. Bremen ordered the ship to flank speed, and the cruiser lurched away from the still waiting life pods and fighters.

"Order the nearest fighters to engage the torpedo. Tell the second squadron to follow the information we will send them and attack the ship."

"Captain," Alex said. "The leader of the second squadron reports they have only enough fuel for about ten minutes of fighting."

"Tell them not to worry. If we do this right, it won't take that long."

Alex almost stood up from his chair. "Captain, the enemy ship is leaving a trail. We can see her inside the space fold. She's jumping toward another fold in space, about one thousand meters to port."

"Bring all guns to bear. Fire at will."

The Paris moved to within optimal firing distance. All four of the ship's turrets trained their massive railguns toward the Sun Lords' ship and opened fire. The high-velocity shells crashed into the hull, gouging huge holes and sending debris and sailors into the vacuum. The enemy ship unleashed a series of mines, which fired individual thrusters, moving toward the Paris. Bremen ordered the remaining fighters and point defense guns to engage the mines as the Paris continued to fire her main guns.

The fighter squadron received updated information from the Paris, and moved into an attack formation and pounded, the until now undetectable ship. Two rounds slammed home and tore a gash in the rear of the ship. The Sun Lord's ship returned fire, her close support guns damaging half of the fighters.

The enemy responded with unbridled fury as the remaining three batteries fired a broadside. Armor-piercing shells ripped away the starboard hanger and destroyed the alpha turret. Bremen ordered a close spread of torpedos, which slammed into the length of the hull, breaking the ship's back and tearing her in two.

Alex turned to Bremen. "Last enemy torpedo is down. We only have eight fighters remaining, and almost all of them are dead in space from lack of fuel."

Bremen gave a slow nod. "Move in close to retrieve our stranded fighters and continue to pick up life pods from the Athens. Did Katrina make it off her ship?"

Alex shook his head. "Her life pod was still onboard when the torpedo hit."

Bremen tapped his console and called up the casualty list. He typed in the following memorandum: Recommend Marines Akio Tanaka and Samuel Rodriguez and Pilot Peter Goodfellow for the Sol Cross, and Alexander Whistler and Captain Katrina Parshikov for meritorious conduct, while engaged against the enemy.

Owen Morgan writes science fiction, fantasy, and alternate history, and lives in the fishing port of Steveston, British Columbia.

Twitter:@owen_morgan1066

BANISHED
BY MARGARET KARMAZIN

My grandmother's name is Haldra and her grandmother's name was Selene and Selene was the wife of Blaine before he left her to download his consciousness into an android body.

It was a new option then and at first only a few did it, but the idea and opportunities spread and soon a fifth of the world's population went for it.

"Never die!" shouted the promotions. "Never suffer disease again!"

"It is the way of the future," Blaine told Selene and anyone else who would listen.

Haldra tells me that his wife was heartbroken. "She fell into a deep depression, and nothing anyone said could relieve her pain. None of the new Methods worked for her, at least for a while, but eventually she healed and went on to become…well, you know what she became."

"A great leader," I said, feeling pride in my ancestors.

"She followed the Methods," Haldra says, "and they changed her into someone new and powerful. It was just the beginning."

She was correct. A miracle combination of Eastern philosophy, chi kung, a then obscure form of yoga and eventually some forms of genetic manipulation gained many followers and eventually spread to most of the world who refused to become android. The practice saved my great-great-grandmother and those who became what is now called Alma, humans with self-control and powers unheard of in former centuries.

"Not only *saved*, but advanced the human race to levels of consciousness then unheard of," I reply, parroting what I had learned in school and from years of Mind Raising with the Elders.

Haldra shoots me a look, half amused, half accusatory. "Don't become too precious," she says. "No one likes precious."

My grandmother is a fierce person, hence her being chosen for this difficult mission, which is about to begin in less than an hour. She has let me accompany her for my education and the privilege of seeing what is left of my great-great grandfather and some other Techs up close. He, like so many others, has lived, if you can call it that for five long generations by changing one android body for another at whim through transference of consciousness. He does not know of my existence, nor of his other descendants, of which there are many, though perhaps not as many as he might imagine. Our people are long lived and limit our reproduction.

At first, the meeting was intended to be virtual, but Haldra convinced the others on the Council that since the event will be monumental, it would be preferable to engage in person.

The Almas and the Techs agreed to use an old playing arena in the neutral zone of old Harare Zimbabwe. The Techs do not need nor desire physical comfort, so the main issue is enough space for them and since only eight Techs will be attending and their current leader reported that only two of his contingent are over 2.4 meters in height or length, Haldra agreed that the field will serve adequately.

We are already seated in a semicircle with me discreetly behind my grandmother. As she so clearly pointed out to me before we arrived,

I am going to be here just to listen and to keep my thoughts to myself. "I don't want to hear even a grunt," she told me.

"But first," I whisper, "what is my great-great-whatever-grandfather's name now? Does he still call himself Blaine?"

"Numbers," Haldra says back, but not out loud. She speaks in my head now, not wanting to disturb our companions who are meditating to raise their courage. "He calls himself DC40-77. He has become a machine."

A black, diamond shape appears in the sky, shoots to our field and stops abruptly. Very much unlike our own ship, one of soft, rotating colors, round and pleasant to the eye. The Tech ship hovers, slides open a large door on its underside and waits. The Almas watch in fascination, murmuring among themselves though I keep quiet as commanded.

***

The ship lowers a ramp, down which seven individuals of various types walk or in one case rolls. A long blue one uses eight legs; another six and the remaining five are variations of human shape. They range in height from 1.5 to 2.2 meters. As I would soon see, DC40-77 and his second in command, ROVOI-11, are among the tallest. All are constructed of a mix of metal and assorted plastics. One looks almost human.

They arrange themselves in a precise semi-circle and direct their attention to the waiting Almas, all staring back in relative fascination.

ROVOI-11 says aloud to DC40-77. "Check them out. I haven't seen one in person for 30.62 years."

The Almas are quite tall themselves, except for me half hidden behind our leader, and dressed in pastel or gray shades of loose clothing.

88

Each of us has carried a small case that opens into a seat and our group moves these to complete a circle with the Techs.

All Almas have a glow about them; one could call it an aura. In some cases, it is difficult to see their features due to the haze of light they emit. The Techs are metallically shiny or soft matte finish, depending on their material and personal grooming. Some of them appear contented, even tranquil as if they are enjoying observing the Almas up close, while others seem distrustful.

Haldra flashes into my questioning mind. "Our ancestor is the tall one in the center, constructed of green and silver materials."

"He has four eyes!" I exclaim.

"They can make themselves however they choose," she says.

"Why does his name consist of numbers?"

"I don't know why," she replies. "I suppose it means something in the Tech world."

***

Haldra opens the meeting. "My friends," she says in her mesmerizing physical voice that could, if she chooses, cause a bird to land out of the sky. "We are here to reach a solution to a difficult problem. The problem being that your own kind are disturbing the natural status quo of the planet and what you are doing to your own land will pull energy from our own. Ours, as you know, depends on a complete balance of life forms, upon a mutual respect between these, while your lifestyle, as it were, clearly shows no interest or concern about the environment. Until now, we have lived in relative harmony since the Great Change, but this harmony is now teetering on the edge of an abyss."

I am proud and amazed by my grandmother, not having seen her before in diplomatic action.

"We don't see why," replies DC4O-77. "We occupy the North and South American landmasses along with Antarctica and keep to our boundaries. We emit nothing poisonous to your life forms of which we are aware. We obviously do not expand our population while you Almas do to a degree, so what's the problem?"

So this *machine* helped to sire my line of humans. I am fascinated and a little bit fearful. And yet there is something about him that seems familiar or comfortable.

"You have moved so far from being human that we are no longer remotely the same species," says Haldra's assistant Macolo. "As a matter of fact, you absolutely do expand your physical presence and now are populating the moon, which was not part of any agreement."

The Techs are silent while bouncing this information among themselves. A small black android who introduces herself as PIRA2.9 speaks. "We saw no reason not to occupy the moon since you Almas have not expressed any interest in doing so."

I feel a wave of emotion from my grandmother. "Our coexistence has depended on trust and respect and we are disappointed that you have bypassed this understanding," she replies.

She gives off an intense and concentrated light that can instill fear in even the largest and strongest of the Techs. Information again flashes among them as they attempt to answer this accusation in a placating manner. I am feeling an odd sympathy and excitement.

"We never thought this would offend you," says DC40-77.

"We never imagined that you would be interested in so dead a sphere," adds ROVOI-11. "Since none of your interests or developments have concerned themselves with such environments in the past."

Haldra is silent for a long moment while she telepathically consults with the other Almas. I can hear some of what she transmits but not all. She has her ways of directing her thoughts exactly where she wants them. Did DC4O-77 and the other Techs fully understand the extent of Alma ability? As we are taught in school, at the beginning of the human division, no one knew where things would lead and even to this day, after centuries of evolution, the two sides understand only a percentage of each other's manner of existence.

"This is the situation," Haldra finally says to the Techs. She pauses, folding her hands and tilting her head back. Her long, black braid that hangs down her back glistens in the sunlight. "When humans made the split with one part going the route of technology and the other the way of the spirit, we naturally did not know where it would lead, did we?"

"It seems to have eventually led to peace, no?" replies what is left of my great-great grandfather.

"Only because we Almas developed the ability to protect and defend ourselves," replies Haldra sharply. "If we had *not* developed such extensive psychic abilities, you Techs would have wiped us off the face of the Earth. Either that or forced us to download our consciousnesses into robotic bodies. We would have had no choice but to surrender and die off as an organic species." She keeps her anger from her voice, but I feel it in my head.

"Perhaps," said ROVOI-11, "though we were not forcing people to do that; those that did, made the choice."

"You are whitewashing the truth," counters Macolo. "At first such a thing was a novelty and voluntary but after only twenty years, it became mandatory with those who refused either desperately trying to escape to our lands or meeting untimely ends. And that was the finale of reproduction for you, wasn't it? Techs can create AI, but they cannot create new human consciousness."

He slowly regards each Tech. "And do you never tire of being in this particular world, DC40-77? How about you, ROVOI-11? You know there are other dimensions, other levels of being, but your kind are forever stuck in this one!"

"Almas *die*," counters DC40-77. "We Techs do not. We can keep going forever if we choose. *And* we can change bodies when we tire of whatever one we currently occupy."

"But we *don't* die," snaps Haldra. "That is where we have passed beyond your understanding. We move, when we choose, to other levels of being. We move out of this universe into others or out of materiality altogether. You are completely unaware of any of this! You are even unaware of two of our kind who are no longer embodied standing among you."

ROVOI-11 and another small blue robot quickly glance about and the blue one switches on a device on his arm.

"I doubt those individuals will be visible in any spectrum of light," says Haldra, a smile in her tone. "Your gadgets are useless."

"Did we come here for you to mock and coerce us?" says DC40-77.

"No," says Haldra. "*We* do not generally force anyone to do anything; we only suggest."

"*Strongly*," said DC40-77. "You 'suggest' *strongly*. And usually there is no way for anyone to go but your way."

My grandmother ignores this even though she must surely know he is correct.

"The present issue is that your kind and my kind have a different view of what's preferable for the planet," she says. "I'm not saying that you destroy the earth now, but you don't *nourish* it. It means little to you whether trees live or not, whether elephants, whales and ants are happy. You do not require oxygen. You care little for beauty. What you seem to desire is intellectual advancement alone."

"What you say is basically so," admits DC40-77.

"We appreciate the beauty of science," says ROVOI-11. "But also, 79W10 here is expert at creating mathematical spiral art in three dimensions."

"Even four," adds 79W10, who apparently cannot resist offering her input. "Visual conjecture, of course," she adds.

Haldra sighs. "I salute your achievement. The issue is that we, being organic, reproduce, though not in the original, primitive manner. We control our propagation but have reached the point where we'd like to do so more than we have. We would like to eventually spread around the globe. Our mental, physical and spiritual health depends upon a healthy living planet and not just in our allotted territories of Asia, Europe, Australia and the Middle East. What you Techs do is affecting all of this."

"What do you want us to do?" asks DC40-77 in obvious exasperation. "The agreement was made and it is not our concern that you now want to expand. We expand also."

"Only with AI," says Haldra sadly. "And everywhere you go, you leave some destruction of life and beauty whether you mean to or not."

"We consider the life of the mind foremost," asserts DC40-77, "and what physical container that occupies is not of concern."

"Here is exactly where we differ," counters my grandmother. "Our minds commune with the nature of this planet, with all that lives upon it, the animals, plants and even the geological layer. You only commune with each other's minds and those are finite."

DC40-77 is silent. There is, in fact, no argument to make. The Techs' supply of human consciousness is, without argument, limited and none are available from we Almas. We have moved far beyond any interest in combining with technology. No Tech would now be stupid enough to try to force us. They learned that a hundred and fifty years prior when, desiring to replenish their supply of human consciousness, they attacked the Alma side on the Asian mainland and were met with an incomprehensible, invisible force. An amazing control of natural energies the Techs had never been able to grasp. And now, DC40-77, apparently remembering, is exuding fear. Any of us can sense it.

After some time, DC40-77 asks, "What do you want? You did not call us here for social intercourse."

"No," says Haldra, almost sadly, "we did not."

"Exactly what then?"

My grandmother consults with Macola and the others. Finally, she answers. "We want you to leave Earth. We want the Earth to ourselves. We have a right to it, since only we can perpetuate the species."

A long silence ensues. "We could destroy you," says DC40-77, though he must sincerely doubt his own words and surely wonders why he has even bothered to make this ridiculous statement.

"We believe not," says Haldra, clearly unfazed. "But think not that we have left you out entirely. There is a way for you and your kind to find happiness and adventure if you are willing."

Suspiciously and with good reason, DC40-77 tilts his large oval head and waits. I watch him and wonder what he was like when he was human.

"We've been so busy over the centuries exploring immaterial realms that we have neglected the third dimension," continues Haldra. "There is much to explore out there and you, with your artificial bodies, are capable of doing that far better than we."

"We already have done some of that," says ROVOI-11 almost peevishly. "Who mapped the worlds in our system? Who is currently building on the moon? Who constructed the base on Mars? It's not our fault the human settlement didn't last. We Techs did everything we could for them."

"And Mars was painfully monotonous," puts in small red GHR7. I can't help but find her appealing and wish I could talk to her.

"Well, you see then," says Haldra, flashing her rather unsettling smile. "What you really need is to venture into deep space. Find unknown worlds and alien cultures. Find a world suitable to your mental and emotional needs and build your own civilization. You don't need an earthlike environment. Perhaps you will even meet creatures who would be interested in joining you and in that way, you could expand as we will do ourselves."

We all look at each other, Almas and Techs. Everyone knows who is really in control and who will obey.

"We will leave you to figure out the best way," finishes my grandmother, and gracefully the Almas rise with me fumbling to stand with them.

"Well," quips DC40-77 after a very long moment, "that went well." Though built of replaceable parts, he has clearly not lost his sense of humor. I would learn later that far back when he was an engineer for the world's largest aircraft company, he'd been known among his fellow humans as "a riot."

The other techs, however, are not amused. "They want us to get out, do they?" grumbles the small red one. "Then let's do it. I've been bored around here anyway."

"You're always bored," comments ROVOI-11.

"It's fun to listen to them," I whisper to my grandmother. She hisses at me to keep quiet.

"Why didn't we do this before anyway?" several Techs mumble at once.

"We'll schedule more meetings," Haldra tells them. "We will help you any way we can."

"Please, Haldra," I say, looking up at her with my eyes as wide and hopefully appealing as possible, "may I meet DC40-77? Just for a moment?"

She gives me a long look before replying. "I am pretty certain that he's not in the mood."

"May I just try, *please?*"

She sighs. "All right, but don't rile him up. He is already quite upset, as are they all. I'll wait right here."

I walk across the grass from our group to theirs, causing most of them to direct their strange and various "eyes" at me. "What's this?" one of them says.

"Please," I say, when I reach them, "I would like to speak with DC40-77."

He seems like a giant to me though he is not much taller than grown Almas, but his android body is thick and wide and looks heavy. "What do you want?" he says.

"Was your name once Blaine Roche?"

A long silence follows while his four white eyes look down at me. "Why do you want to know?" he finally answers.

I swallow and say, "I am your great-great-granddaughter."

"Oh," he says simply, "Oh."

Do I imagine that he is a bit "choked up?" His metal and plastic arms surround me and hold me while we both murmur many things. Inside, he is still as human as he ever was.

***

At one of the many meetings that follow - Haldra permits me to attend a few of them - someone, not DC40-77 though he is quickly onboard, presents the idea of downloading themselves directly into starships to save space and materials.

"Once we find a place to our liking, we can dismantle the ships and use them and materials from the new world to build ourselves bodies. During the voyage, some of us will stay in separate form to perform manual labor and maneuvers onboard. We can take turns occupying those forms."

DC40-77 puts together a team to design the new ships, never having lost his human craving for adventure and possibly having needed this push. Haldra and the other Almas allow me to spend time with him while he and his associates build the fabulous vehicles. I hear them joking and discussing their lives. In no way have they lost who they are.

"It is a crime to send them away," I tell my grandmother and whoever will listen but neither she nor they change their minds. I imagine becoming one of them and going with them.

"Use the Methods," she tells me. "Meditate more. Spend time with trees and animals and water. Commune with the sky and the fields. You will remember who you are."

I do as she suggests and yes, eventually I get it. I look into the eyes of a dog, a deer in the forest, a lizard in my lap; I feel the sun on rocks, hear the trees whispering among themselves, the stream gurgling to itself and yes, I understand.

The ships leave our world fifteen months later. There is some bitterness on the part of some Techs, though not all. "It is time," says my great-great-grandfather.

We, a large group of Almas, are there to witness their takeoff. DC40-77 is no longer in the body I grew to know, but downloaded into the third ship to leave. He has left me a gift.

I open it after the ships have gone. It consists of a black photo viewer of an antique design. The object charges from the sun. You tap a button and one photo at a time stands up in holographic 3D. The first one is of a young woman with her young man holding a baby. My eyes fill with tears since I instantly know that this is Selene and Blaine and my great grandmother as an infant. This is who he once was.

I look up at the bright blue sky and my heart goes with them into the blackness of space.

Margaret Karmazin's credits include stories published in literary and national magazines, including Rosebud, Chrysalis Reader, North Atlantic Review, Mobius, Confrontation, Pennsylvania Review, Cloaked Press, The Speculative Edge and Another Realm. Her stories in The MacGuffin, Eureka Literary Magazine, Licking River Review and Mobius were nominated for Pushcart awards. Her story, "The Manly Thing," was nominated for the 2010 Million Writers Award. She has stories included in several anthologies, including STILL GOING STRONG, TEN TWISTED TALES, PIECES OF EIGHT (AUTISM ACCEPTANCE), ZERO GRAVITY, DAUGHTERS OF ICARUS and SPACE BETWEEN STARS. She has also published a YA novel, REPLACING FIONA, a children's book, FLICK-FLICK & DREAMER and a collection of short stories, RISK.

EXECUTIVE MATERIAL
BY GARY WOSK

Erwin Puddles looked at his watch and yawned. It was only eight in the morning, the beginning of another long, boring day on the job at the struggling confectionary company.

An employee who worked in the marketing team for fifteen years, the meek Erwin, whose surname was a perfect fit because of his weak bladder, held out hope that he would be given more work. His co-workers couldn't care less. They just went through the motions. Not Erwin. He longed to climb the ladder of success and earn his critical parents' approval, but the problem was no one took him seriously, especially his boss.

He nearly jumped out of his socks when the voice came over the PA system. Perhaps it wouldn't be such a monotonous day after all. Maybe, just maybe, everyone would be asked to evacuate the building. Yes, a fire drill, that would be a nice change of pace.

"Attention, all workers. This is Barbara Ganoosh in your HR department. The efficiency experts from Quigley Systems have arrived. Do not be alarmed. Go about your work. Everything will be fine. Please wear your special glasses when evaluated to protect your eyes from the light. And remember, always be honest. They know when you're not being truthful. On behalf of the Suzie Sweets Company, thank you very much for your cooperation. Good luck."

Efficiency experts. Oh, no, they'll let me go, Erwin thought. On the other hand, maybe he'd be better off if they terminated there on the spot, he ruminated. Sure, he earned a decent living, had good health coverage and would one day have a nice pension, but he was rotting away. Maybe working as a minimum wage greeter at a big box retail store like Costco would be more gratifying than sitting around eating samples of coconut cream truffles all day.

A few moments after the announcement, Erwin's boss, Arthur Crowley, the director of marketing, came bolting out of his office with a determined look on his face. Once a hardworking employee who would regularly visit the CEO and make one suggestion after the other, he was now a shadow of his former self. Now instead of developing marketing campaigns, he developed plans for his next vacation. Arthur had become a bitter, slow-thinking snail who would arrive on the job late and leave early. Often, the door to his office would remain closed.

With the announcement that came over the PA system, Arthur, at least momentarily, snapped out of his malaise. This was a chance to reassert himself. "I hope everyone heard that," he hollered. "Let's gather in my office in a few minutes for a quick meeting. We've got to figure out what we've been doing lately. I estimate we'll have about twenty minutes to iron everything out before the efficiency experts arrive."

"Can we take a break first?" sheepishly suggested Glen, whose favorite pastime was playing solitaire against the computer.

"That's preposterous," retorted Arthur. You just started your day of doing nothing. If it wasn't for your connections, I would have fired you a long time ago. Now get your lame ass in my office."

It had been a while since the staff had assembled in Arthur's office, but then, as always, they only focused on company business for a few minutes. Their attention quickly turned to something more important, the group lottery ticket. They'd fantasize about what they would do right if they won millions of dollars. There was always, "I'll give those bastards two hours' notice if I win" or "Why wait so long?" And better yet, "We don't owe them anything. We've given them the best years of our lives by doing nothing."

As he waited for the members of his staff to arrive in his office, Arthur finished gargling with mouth wash. He then placed the Listerine in the top drawer of his desk next to the half-consumed bottle of Johnny Walker.

Once everyone was seated in front of his desk, Arthur snuffed out his cigar in an ash tray located next to his computer. It was against company policy to smoke on the job, but what the heck, he figured, if they caught him, fine. They'd just slap him on the wrist. He then pushed aside stacks of dusty documents, lifted his legs and lowered them on his desk, and said, "Well, here we are everyone. D-Day has arrived. We will soon find out if they let us keep our jobs or declare us obsolete. We have a tough fight on our hands because we haven't done a damn thing in a while."

Out of the blue, Arthur began to reminisce about the past. "I remember when we used to deal with human efficiency experts. Real people. It would take weeks to evaluate everyone. Now it's done within a few hours by these light beings. Oh, how I miss the days when it was easy to mislead people into thinking you were necessary. You can't fool these light beings. They're sharp I tell you. They'll size you up before you know it and declare you duplicative, non-value added. So, there's no reason to worry. You'll all be gone soon. But I digress."

Arthur turned to Erwin, the staff member he liked to pick on the most. "What have you been up to besides twiddling your thumbs?"

"Research."

"Research? I don't think so. You're doing what we all do. Nothing. Don't pretend to be better than the rest of us you little milquetoast."

"I'm sorry, sir," said Erwin, "but don't you remember asking me to write a report about the marketing strategies of our competitors and suggest a new approach for our company?"

"Don't be insolent you little mealy-mouthed weasel."

"I mean no disrespect Mr. Crowley."

After resting his interlocked hands underneath his chin with his index fingers touching his lip for about ten seconds, he finally confessed. "Oh, yes, that. I vaguely remember asking you to write the report, but that was two years ago. Where is it? What's taken so long?"

"I finished the report months ago, but every time I try to make an appointment with you to discuss my findings you say, 'Later, Erwin, later. I'm busy right now.'"

Arthur wasn't about to allow this underling embarrass him in front of his staff.

"If you had any back bone, you'd have knocked on my door and just walked in, like those other bastards. No one respects my privacy around you, so why should you? You're as meek as they come."

"I did walk in on you that one time, Mr. Crowley. Remember? You were totally immersed in something that was happening on your computer screen. People without hardly anything on, contorting, making funny sounds. You told me to scram."

"Still talking back? That's enough, Erwin. If you have to know, it was an educational video that HR had sent me," Arthur said with a straight face. "And you can watch it with me Erwin when you enter puberty."

"Mature audiences only," chimed in Victor. "Right, boss?"

The staff continued to snicker and asked for more details about the video.

"It was about the dangers of forming workplace romances," Arthur said with a wink.

Hysterical laughter broke out.

"Okay everyone. Calm down," said Arthur, trying to restore order. "How about you Oscar? What have you been doing to help the company? Whenever I walk past your cubicle it looks like you're in a coma."

Like the others who would be posed the same question, he responded with a blank stare. Nothing of course came to mind.

With the light beings only minutes away, Arthur had to quickly develop a strategy.

"Everyone except Erwin should get lost. Leave the building. Go sightseeing. Jump on a tour bus. Go for a long walk. Have breakfast again. Maybe go home sick. The flu is going around. Whatever."

"Leave?" asked Johnson, still annoyed at the disruption of his usual morning nap. "I was looking forward to lunch. The cafeteria is serving franks and beans today."

"I'll text everyone when it's safe to return," said Arthur who then burped. "If they ask where everyone is, I'll just say everyone is visiting our retail stores today We'll see if that flies. If not, well, it was nice not working with you."

The staff fell silent. The thought of having to find a real job without much to show for themselves as employees of the Suzie Sweets Company terrified them.

Conceding that Arthur's plan for them to get lost was their best option, everyone except for Erwin, nodded their heads in agreement.

"Okay, Erwin," Arthur said after the others had left his office. "I'd like to go over that report with you when the efficiency experts arrive. Maybe that will save our jobs. Bring the report to my office right away. They'll be here soon. We can make believe we're having a serious conversation."

That's when Erwin's weak bladder acted up again.

"I need to use the lavatory," said Erwin apologetically.

"Not again, Erwin. Bad timing, Erwin. Bad timing. If they find you in the lavatory, you're dead meat."

"I can't help it. I have to go bad."

"Do what you want. You're an imbecile. Be quick. I'm counting on you for once."

And Erwin did make it quick, but not quick enough. The light beings were waiting for him in the hallway just outside the lavatory.

"Stop," commanded a voice. "You there. Stop. Protect your eyes from the brightness. Put on your glasses."

"Me?" asked Erwin.

"Yes, you. Identify yourself, please."

"My name is Erwin Puddles."

"I am Quigley and this is my associate Quigley."

Erwin looked puzzled.

"Yes, we both have the same name and say the same things at the same time. We reside in a computer and mere projections."

With his glasses on, Erwin could barely make out the outlines of two human being entities.

"The scanning has begun. State your department and role?" the Quigleys said together.

"I work in the marketing department. I am an associate manager."

"How long have you been an associate manager."

"Ten years."

"That is a long time to be an associate manager. Why haven't you been promoted?

"You'll have to ask my boss.

"What is his name?

"Arthur Crowley."

The light of the efficiency experts began to dim, which wasn't a good sign. They sensed that Erwin wasn't happy.

"What do you do? Others in the company have had some difficulty in answering this question."

"I develop marketing campaigns, well, I should say, I used to develop marketing campaigns, but it's been slow lately."

"It shouldn't be slow, Erwin Puddles. Your company is on the verge of bankruptcy."

"Yeah, that's what I've heard."

The lights began to flicker

"That's seems like a rather complacent response. What are you going to do about it?"

"I've been trying to do something about it for about two years now."

The Quigleys were confounded.

"What are you talking about, Erwin Puddles?"

"My boss asked me to write a report how to make our company more profitable."

"Have you finished this report?"

"Yes. My boss and I were supposed to review the report when you, I mean, both of you, arrived, but then I had to take care of this other business."

"Other business."

"Uh, use the lavatory."

The efficiency experts were clearly irritated at Crowley.

That's inexcusable," they said. "What are you holding in your hands, Erwin Puddles?"

"A yellow legal sized writing pad."

"For what purpose?"

"I was jotting down notes for another report I would like to work on."

"While using the lavatory?"

"Well, I know this sounds crazy, that's where I do my best thinking. It's just amazing."

"Erwin Puddles. You are very interesting."

The beams of lights were brighter now than ever, which was a good sign.

"The evaluation is nearly complete," said the Quigleys. "Before we let you go however, we have one more question to ask you."

"Let me go? That's what I expected," said Erwin rejectingly. "I tried to do a good job, but no one would listen."

"We are not letting you go. Tell us about what your boss is working on?"

Erwin remained mute.

The lights became dimmer.

"You don't' have to say a thing Erwin Puddles. We know the answer."

"Are we done now?"

"Yes, the scanning is complete," said the Quigleys. "Our research indicates that the best thinkers in business spend a considerable amount of time in the lavatory as you seem to do. And because your work may be very important to the company, we have decided to retain you as an employee. You no longer will have to report to Arthur Crowley."

"I'm being transferred?"

"No. He is out."

"Where is he going?"

"Possibly to maintenance, if they'll have him."

"And me?

"You, Erwin Puddle, have been promoted to chief executive officer."

Erwin had finally climbed the ladder of success.

Gary Wosk was raised in the Bronx and Los Angeles. Since graduating from California State University, Northridge he has been a newspaper reporter and spokesperson. He currently works in the field of media relations and is a member of the California Writers Club in the San Fernando Valley.

IT STARTS WITH A PROMISE
BY BOB RITCHIE

I

Tandy cannot see the floor and wonders why. She waits, watches the electric-blue neon sky count seconds. At every seventh pulse, it changes color.

"Down. I should look down again." Tandy's voice comes to her as if traveling through three feet of turbulent water. But she looks down and notes, "Still no floor. I suppose I'm not surprised." Silent in suspension, Tandy feels her thoughts as they run like candle wax through the nooks and crannies of her mind. "Down, see what I see. If not a floor, what? Does it matter?"

Tandy cannot see the floor. The linoleum, gray and spotted with blotches of freshly spit baby food, has receded into a distance that shares few similarities with "space." She studies the shifting landscape below. No floor. But her brain begins to perceive patterns. And it is like when distant letters swim into place as you approach; become words you can understand. It is a maze, there below. Not suspended in the air. Hung up on nothing. Supported by an immeasurable void. She makes a small mental leap and realizes that she too is hung up on nothing.

Tandy looks up. Her eyes confirm the existence of the pulsing, alien sky, though some sense tells her it may be a convenient fiction of her mind to keep her rational.

"Well anyway, it's all very pretty."

Something below moves, and Tandy focuses on the blur. In the maze she makes out figures, stumbling and awkward. They run headlong into the maze's walls but stand right up and scurry off, only to trip over each other again. Crying, pleading, they beg the sky.

Tandy clears the falling wave of sun-streaked brown hair from her eyes and stifles a laugh, thinking she must be heartless to find humor in their plight. "It's just that they look so funny—like mechanical dolls running and running and never arriving."

"Hello." A Voice. It comes wrapped in a delicious, spreading warmth that rushes up and down her legs and beneath her short cotton nightie. Her nipples stand at attention. Voice and warmth, together, but separate; they invade her tiny, private universe. Something like heated oil that soothes and balms. And these new inputs shove the maze and its inhabitants from her mind.

"Hello?" It is a lush bass sound like the deepest tone of a tremendous pipe organ. It makes her tremble and excites her almost to orgasm. She smells vanilla and honey. Her flesh contracts as if from a wave of cold. But she isn't cold, not at all!

"I don't know who you are," she starts, but even as the first syllables leave her mouth, she thinks, *don't I?* The question stops her, but no answer slides past her open ears. She starts again, "I don't know who you are, but you could play God on TV." Without thought, she strokes a sensitive area on her left hip. More gooseflesh.

"Thank you." The Voice chuckles to itself and continues. "We've been watching you. . . ." A flash of violet lights the . . . aboveness. Two flashes. On the seventh, violet changes to chartreuse and the vanilla and honey scent becomes stronger. With a touch of fresh ground pepper.

Tandy stays her hand and takes a deep breath before asking, "Who?"

Silence. A pause that stretches. Tandy doesn't mind; that warm-oil feeling is too good to even think about stressing out.

The Voice repeats, "We've been watching you." A pause before the Voice continues, "That scene with Myron the other night was a little out there, but other than that, we think that it is time."

Oh my goodness, 1984! "What do you know about Myron and me?" Tandy demands, embarrassed. A faint rose creeps into her pale cheeks.

A rubber-chicken and a pair of spaghetti handcuffs materialize from the nothing.

Blushing a deeper shade of red than before, Tandy explains, "It was all good, clean fun."

The sex toys fade away.

"'Fun,' we'll believe." But the Voice holds no touch of reprimand, nothing that could be called disgust or displeasure. In fact, it seems on the edge of laughter and some great joy too huge to imagine. "We think that you are more than ready. Even if you are a touch kinky. And . . . wait." Another pause. Tandy has the feeling that the Voice is conferring with others. It comes back, "Fact is, we could use some frivolity around here. Eternity grates after the first thousand years or two."

Tandy begins to expand, to fill the nothing around her. The maze below her grows distant and Tandy has the nagging feeling that she's forgotten something. Her bare toes wriggle in the void. "What's happening?"

"You are moving on."

"But I have a son." she objects, remembering past the luscious

Voice.

"Don't worry." Again, Tandy has the feeling that she *knows* this voice. With more time, she might attach a name, *Father, Brother, Friend.* Its identity revolves around a promise made long ago and then occulted. Sort of.

"Come," it commands.

She vibrates in its grasp. "I haven't got a thing to wear!" She wails. "And my son? . . ."

"You will speak to him one last time." Then Voice hums, and it is like a warm washcloth blotting her forehead. It murmurs to her and becomes a thousand, a million, an infinity of smaller Voices. They comfort her but cannot abolish her worry.

My son.

II

Paul cannot see his mother and feels sad; it is a sadness of 15 years. With time, the mind's eye grows cataracts, and to an 18-year-old boy, 15 years is an eternity. He stares at the ceiling and the words "I promise" come to his lips without his realizing.

A long time. A long time to live with everyone's stories about one Tandara Drey, his mother. He knows the "facts": She abandoned him at age three, leaving him with only a photograph and his favorite teddy bear; he never knew his father; after having been left, Paul almost died from malnutrition before someone found him, crying in an empty, cold apartment. He knows all the facts.

Objectively, logically, they all added up to one thing. Can't really deny that.

Still, try as he might, Paul cannot hate his mother, cannot do the simple arithmetic that would equal "criminal bitch" in any other person's ethical universe. He remembers the orphanage, the state homes and foster parents (replace *home* with *jail; parents* with *jailers*), the name-calling. He remembers it all. Especially the name-calling, as that still continues today in the youth camp. Bad enough being a bastard, but an *abandoned* bastard! . . .

Paul cannot hate his mother. He stopped trying a long time ago. But he wishes that he could remember her, call fond memories to his inner eye.

He pulls out the photograph and stares at her again. He contemplates the small woman captured therein: long, brown, sun-bleached hair and a fine-featured face; she almost looks like a young boy. Still, Paul sees undeniable beauty. Overlaying that, he sees a tranquility that he has yet to find in any other person. He sees in the picture some of what the mirror shows him every morning when he runs a comb through his own short hair. "My Dad must have been a little bigger," he muses for the umpteenth time. Paul stands at 5'11" and has the wide shoulders of a football player. But after all his study, it's no good. He cannot see his *mother,* only a Polaroid, colors fading.

He shrugs the wide shoulders and tucks the photograph into the breast pocket of his Pendleton shirt. Today, Paul is celebrating his 18th birthday. *Whoopdeedoo.* He twirls his finger in the air. He sits in his room and stares at the faded green bedspread covering the narrow twin bed. He's stayed in the youth camp for over three years. Through ups and downs. Mostly downs in the last couple of weeks. Not the people who run the camp; they've always treated him okay. It's the other kids, *two* other kids.

Paul likes to do his own stuff, not bother other people. And for some reason, that twists the skulls of Louann and her boyfriend Juke. It isn't just name-calling anymore. Last month, they reset his alarm to wake him up at 4 AM one day and then 10 AM the next (making him late for work). The latest "joke" was a bucket of water over his door. Paul had never seen that in real life, just on TV.

Though never having been the paranoid sort, it seems to Paul that those two were put on this earth just to make him suffer. And they had a way of involving everyone, of making all the kids take part in their cruelties.

Well, not Gina, he amends. He nods to himself, a grin displacing his unhappy frown. He passes a square, dish-water-hardened hand over his face to erase the smile. *Can't think about Gina now.* He rubs the corners of his eyes, not wanting to deal with tears at the moment.

Paul has—had, until he quit this same afternoon—a job, so he has some money. He'll be taking off today, with few reasons stronger than instinct. Two, really. The first? He wants to leave his small history behind, so no one can hold it against him, so that if he meets someone on the street, no preconceived notions will get in the way. He wants to lose himself in the present. As those Alcoholics Anonymous folks say, "One day at a time." *Good saying,* Paul thinks, *it helps preserve that old anonymity.*

But the primary impetus for his get-gone actions is the pulling. It started when he was a kid. Constant, but not overwhelming. At the end of last August, everything changed; the insistent tugs started getting stronger and more constant. Now, with Christmas around the corner and the chilling frost of autumn deepening to out-and-out cold, the tugs won't be ignored or denied and have, in fact, escalated to yanks.

Paul looks at the dresser on the opposite wall. A bus ticket to the city of his birth sits on the imitation wood. *My birthplace.* He savors the words in his mind. And they taste so good that he says them aloud, allowing their flavor to burst upon his tongue, "My birthplace." The place from where his mother disappeared. Paul has a need to search for this woman and stand before her. His grail is not confrontation, only the vision of her. He wants a real memory.

He picks up the old teddy bear that has always traveled with him from place to place. "Well Roof, I think I'm going to leave you behind on this one. I want to find my mom. Ask her why. I know she must have had a good reason."

Rufus, as usual, does not speak. His brown button eyes stare up at Paul, but, unlike when he was a child, they don't hold any answers for him.

"I'm 18 now," he explains, "time to conquer the world." He laughs to himself . . . *at* himself, feeling a buoyancy that the facts should not support. "I don't know her name, her past, or even her favorite color, but I do know I can find her." Looking out the window, Paul sees Gina and the Tiller Twins coming through the gate. Louann and Juke, Paul assumes, are still at the hamburger joint where Louann is a cashier and Juke flips burgers and makes passes at the other cashiers. The youth camp encourages their charges to work and save money. Some of the kids say that doing so is just a way to get rid of them. But Paul isn't so cynical. He believes that the policy helps prepare the camp's wards for the real world.

The shouts and laughter of younger children playing dodge ball on the asphalt playground reach him through the open window. Paul feels a momentary sadness. He's leaving behind the only real home he ever had. And Gina.

He shakes his head and sets Rufus on the pillow, then moves him over to the dresser, saying, "Green isn't your color, eh, old guy? Pseudo-wood suits you much better." He looks out the curtainless window again: Gina, long black hair swaying with her walk, catches his look and lifts her head. She smiles with a pure clean joy that makes Paul ache. Seeing her, so alive, it forces him to think about what he is doing to her. She waves a gloved hand. He waves back, smiles, thinks about leaving a note. He remembers the salt taste of her neck after walking home from school. The ache grows and localizes itself square in the center of his heart. *Maybe I could stay. . . .*

The tug. Definable. Once tiny, now, not. Paul *feels* it. He remembers the first time it came—at the Sullivan place down on Cayle Street. Paul was only six-and-a-half when old man Sullivan put the moves on him. That pull, that sense of being connected to a *puller* made him strong, made it possible for him to act, rather than freeze in fear.

Paul had punched Mr. Sullivan in his exposed privates (all wrinkled and hairy and, *ugh*. . . . Remembering still made him shiver.), and then he had run. Not far. Down the street to a yellow house with a low brick wall in front. At first, the young couple within had expressed doubt, but had acquiesced to Paul's crying request and called Social Services instead of old man Sullivan. Two days later, it had all come out. Apparently Sullivan had been abusing children for almost 22 years, and not one of them had said a word. Until Paul.

It's that tug, that connectivity that tells Paul he will find his mother. Didn't it keep him from going on the field trip in seventh grade? (The bus hit a hot dog: a seven-foot billboard that hadn't been anchored well against the wind. The bus spun out on the mustard and three kids and the driver died; six more kids were injured along with the teacher. The driver died because he was picking his nose: The impact sent the finger up into his brain. Paul went to the teacher's funeral. He'd liked her. It was a good ceremony, but all that rich food gave him gas.)

He remembers when the connection saved more than his physical life: Mid-Terms last year had been a bitch and a half. At the precise moment that he decided he would have to take Mel up on his offer and buy the test instead of study, he felt a powerful urge to sit his ass down and crack open the books. After successfully fighting the compulsion off, he heard—literally *heard* (as in sound waves transmitted to the ear, received by his brain, and turned into a message)—a growled, "or else!" He sat, he cracked, he studied. He called himself Caesar, but no one laughed because they didn't understand the allusion.

That night of unplanned schoolwork was supposed to have been his first date with Gina Marino (new to the camp and Sidville Senior High, both). She hadn't minded when he told her he had to study. She wasn't—isn't—a bad person. He'd made it up to her later.

The connection. Paul was the pulled, but who was the puller? All he had to do was trace it back.

The fading sun hovers over the three-story girls' dorm across the yard of the camp. It illuminates the dusty, fading bricks, and Paul sees them as they must have appeared back when the camp was still a newly built, low-power TV station: the earth-red wall with its internal glow of newness, not yet wearing the city pall of smoke and dust. He blinks and the girls' dorm is back in its place. Paul watches Gina enter the building. Familiar with her habits, he knows he has about 45 minutes while she showers the day's work from her budding, already voluptuous body. Then she'll head over.

"I better get gone." Paul grabs up his suitcase (the one with the cracked leather handle that he'd found in the Gingham's attic; that had been a nice enough place. No tugs. But no real desire to stay, neither on his nor the older couple's part) and heads for the door. His roommate isn't in, which makes leaving easier. Chris is a good-hearted, dramatic guy and would want to turn Paul's leave-taking into an event of epic proportion.

"See ya, Roof."

The bear stares, solemn as a priest.

* * *

The city frightens Paul at first. The bus trip was too short a journey to really prepare him mentally for life in something other than a small town. And anyway, how does one prepare for the utterly alien?

Standing on the sidewalk in front of a grease-smeared glass window that reads "Bill's Café," Paul looks across the street and sees the words "Help Wanted" in the window of a shoe store. A boot-shaped sign hanging over the door sways, pushed by the light, coldish breeze. Paul shoves his hands as deep as they'll go into the pockets of his down jacket. He shifts from foot to foot for a moment, glad he'd thought to put on his heavy wool socks but regretting the fact that he'd left his gloves behind. Checking the "Help Wanted" sign again, he comes to a decision and speaks into the chill air. "Need a place to stay and a place to work. And lunch. Might be able to take care of those last two right now." He watches the street, waiting for a break in the traffic. When the light a half block down changes to red, the street empties; he starts across.

The pull! It yanks him with an urgency he's rarely felt. Paul dashes across the street and into the nearest open door. Behind him, a heavy rumble shakes the street as a cement mixer, barrel spinning, speeds by. Paul feels the wind of it on his back. He shakes his head, wondering how he could have *not* seen a truck! Absently, he dusts his hands off on his newer pair of 501s.

"Boy was you lucky, kid." The voice startles Paul, and he jumps a little as he turns to face its source. "Fookin truck almost made beans on toast outta ye! What's the matter, then? New ta the city? Yea. Ye got the look: no grease on yer noggin."

He is a tall man, sporting a mustache and a derby. His shoulders slump, as if in defeat. Paul, who watched "A Fish Called Wanda" so many times that the videotape wore out, decides that the man before him looks and sounds a lot like John Cleese, the English actor. Except he has bad teeth, a crooked thumb, and—Paul looks around himself with eyes open wide—he seems to be the proprietor of a porn store. A layer of rancid oil seems to coat the face before him.

The man remembers his duty and pulls away from Paul, "Wait 'ere a sec. You 18?"

Paul, still stunned from his narrow escape, nods, gulps once, and says, "Ye-yes sir. Today."

The man takes Paul by the elbow with a long-fingered hand and leers, "So, 'ow can I be of service to ye?" A light (old man Sullivan) in the man's eyes makes Paul shudder and try to remove his elbow. The hand is strong, making Paul wonder whether the weak posture might be a kind of disguise.

Unable to free himself, Paul pulls back as much as he can and tells the man, "Oh, I don't . . . I'm looking for my mother?"

The tall shopkeeper smiles and opens his thin lips to make some sort of crude remark. But a startled look of recognition runs down from his eyes and chases the smile away. The creepy, old-man-Sullivan light winks out, as if switched off. Letting go of Paul's elbow, the man reaches into his pocket and removes a small, black leather-bound book. Its pages are torn and the corners ragged as if from having been turned down many times. While thumbing through the worn volume, the man mumbles to himself in a voice remarkably free of accent. "'Oh, I don't . . . I'm looking . . .' I know it's in here! 'Pardon my butt, can you give . . .' No, no, wrong continuum."

Paul watches, unsure of what he is seeing, hearing. He decides to exit now and eliminate the possibility of a problem. He turns on his heel, but at the sound of sliding sneaker on stained floor, the man shoots a hand out and recaptures Paul's elbow, saying, "Hold on there, I found it!"

The fellow reads for several seconds. His lips move. When he finishes, he lifts his eyes out of the small book and stares into Paul's eyes. Something—very deep—like age, but . . . bigger. Paul wonders how he ever could have seen something strange in those eyes. Not enough room for anything else but the . . . whatever, in there. Though still unsure and nervous, Paul doesn't try to pull away. The two of them stand—as if frozen by a camera's demanding lens. Outside, the light has changed, and traffic sounds roar through the open door.

The man slips the small book back into his pocket; he steps around Paul to close the door, muting the snarls of the passing vehicles. When he assumes his place before Paul, his posture is erect, his shoulders no longer bowed. Sliding back his blue-striped shirtsleeve, the man consults his watch. "You were 26 seconds late," he says, in a crisp, clear voice. Definitely, the English accent has disappeared. He continues, "But that can be overlooked. Call me GA. I'll be helping you in the transition."

The man, GA, wears an expectant look. Paul notes that not only has he shed the accent (and isn't there something familiar about that voice?), but also the palpable sliminess that masqueraded as innocent sweat. A disguise.

"Transition?"

Using Paul's shoulder as a rudder, GA steers the boy deeper into the store saying, "Come. We must hurry: Though 26 seconds doesn't seem like much, we'll be cutting it close."

Bewildered beyond resistance, Paul lets himself be led through a maze of lewd, often unpleasant merchandise. Pictures, magazines, posters, neckties, dogtoys. They take a wrong turn and run headlong into a rack labeled "Prick Pleasers." Rack, man, and new man all crash to the floor, accompanied by diverse thuds and thumps. GA leaps to his feet and then hauls Paul up by the elbow, hustling him ever deeper into the store. The things they pass: videos, gag gifts, stickers. Paul's eyes goggle.

After another wrong turn—and how can such a small store be so big?—they reach an oasis of visual calm. They enter a room with

white, bare walls and a small desk, top lightly spiced with paper.
Nothing more to stimulate the senses. Paul turns to GA and asks,
"What did you mean, by '26 seconds late' and all that?"

"You were expected, Paul," he says between gasps. The tone of
his voice suggests that the answer is obvious. "You wish to find your
mother, do you not?" With one hand, GA indicates the chair. The other,
he puts to his heart, like an old man checking his pulse. *But he can't be
more than 30,* Paul thinks.

Shrugging mental shoulders, Paul takes the chair. Now GA
towers over him like a second-grade teacher. "Yes, I told you that," he
answers, then asks, "*Who* expected me?"

GA leans against the wall and gulps air to calm his wheezing.
After a moment, he fishes out the black book, riffles its pages with his
thumb (no longer crooked). To Paul, it looks like one of the small books
of the New Testament that they gave him when he got to the camp.

"You are traveling, Paul," says GA, ignoring the question.
"You've been traveling—toward your mother—every time you obeyed
those little tugs."

Paul touches his breast pocket, where resides the picture of his
mother. He'd never told anyone about that. Not even Gina. "How do
you know about those?" he demands.

GA smiles, and his face changes. Long wrinkles fissure his long
features. *No, not 30.* The smile folds them all in and around each other
until his face is crisscrossed with lines. "Sometimes the tugs were bits of
prescience—warnings of one sort or another. Sometimes they were
nothing more than backups to your own developing conscience. You
listened to your conscience—most of the time, even if you needed the

odd persuasion. That was my job." His smile broadens before he continues; the wrinkles acquire depth, like cracks in the earth. "You paid attention more than most people do, I'm happy to say."

"Great," Paul leans forward in the chair, "but you still haven't explained: Who expected me?" Though patient for a teenager, Paul still feels the tall man is giving him too much unnecessary information. His hands go out as if to pull what he wants from GA.

"*We* expected you, Paul." As if that fully answers the question. GA taps on Paul's forearm. "I want you to listen to something."

In the air, a child's voice floats. Paul feels as if he should recognize it. And it stirs something in him. A memory? He isn't sure.

"Mama? Where are you? I can't see you?" A pause. A small dog barks, and someone curses far in the background, then, "Yes, Mama, I promise. I miss you. Bye bye, Mama."

Remembrance falls on Paul like a spring shower. He had been talking to his mother, promising to obey her instructions and guidance . . . and her warnings. How could he have forgotten?

He jumps up, grabs GA by the wrist. "I get it. She never abandoned me! My mother is the tug. Like a guardian angel or something." Excited? You bet!

"Or something." GA nods, agreeing, then adds, "And not just your mother; *all* of us." His smile expands again until it looks as if the corners of his mouth are going to reach around and connect in the back of his head. Maybe if they do, the top of his skull will flip back like a Pez dispenser. Paul stifles a giggle at the thought.

A fluorescent light flickers, making a small ticking sound. Paul releases the tall man's wrist and begins to pace in the small room. For the first time, Paul notices how warm it is. His down jacket makes him hot enough that beads of sweat pop out on his broad forehead. He turns on GA "You have to help me find her." He stops. "But, she *is* dead, then. Angels aren't alive." Not a question.

GA hasn't stopped nodding until this point. He rubs his finger across his chin and says, "Well, I wouldn't put it *that* way, but it doesn't matter. You've reached the end of this line, son. It's time to pass into a new plane of existence." His face seems to shift as he speaks.

Paul stares as GA's features become one person, then another, and again, repeating. It seems that somewhere in there is his mother, though Paul can't be sure.

"I'm going to die? What, are you the Grim Reaper?" He takes a step back and hears the lonely scuff of his tennis shoes on the cement floor. Suddenly he's cold again.

GA chuckle/s to himself/themselves, features stopping at middle-aged Caucasian with too long sideburns. "Let me explain something. Death is not the black side of white. In fact, when a person is said to be *dead,* either one of two things is happening: recycling or growth." As an aside, he adds, "Those Catholics never did get it right."

Paul blinks. "I don't think I understand."

"Recycling: The soul leaves the body and goes into a sort of holding tank. When it's next up, it enters another—newborn—body. A soul can be recycled a million times and never learn its lessons, never *grow.* Sad when that happens." GA frowns and shakes his head. He's bald, now, and has a mustache; a tiny scar divides the left half of his upper lip in half. Paul searches his memory for the prior version of GA but comes up blank.

He shakes off the small confusion and after letting the pause stretch for one second more than he can take, prompts, "What about growth?"

GA's smile lights his face again, "Yes. *Growth* is when the soul is ready to move on. To grow into a new plane of existence. Your soul is ready to go. You've done well in the past few lives."

"The past *few?*"

"It's a cumulative thing," explains GA. He checks his watch again, "I need to cut this short. Must make up those 26 seconds. I've another customer due in."

Paul cannot speak. He lets hang his mouth as an aura of golden light surrounds GA. Inexplicably, Paul smells vanilla and honey. Maybe with the lightest dusting of black pepper.

"Come along then. Mustn't tarry."

The light grows very bright above Paul's head. It seems to have gravity. It pulls. At the same time, he feels sleepy. A warmth slips over his body. Seductive and beckoning. Gina's face blooms on GA's; a melancholy as thick as cold fog settles on Paul's consciousness.

"Wait," he says, "what about? . . ." The fog threatens to overcome the warmth. Cold and matchless like a void.

GA answers in Gina's voice, "It's the only real downside to the process: To everyone here, on Earth, you have to be dead." GA looks solemn and his face—Gina!—stretches. He adds, "You'll be able to give a message to the next, um, candidate, but it won't be consciously remembered." The eyes. *Her* eyes.

Paul is nodding, answering the not-question before it comes. Which it then does (but from a *new* face, one that reminds Paul

125

of all the old movie heroes): "I assume that would be Gina?"

Nodding and nodding and the muscles of his neck are soft taffy. The fog lifts, slowly at first, then as the light above and the smell of vanilla and honey (and a touch of black pepper) all around him strengthens, the warmth folds him into itself like cheese into a cooking omelet. Paul hears an odd, wordless chant that sounds farther than the other side of the pulsing, violet sky above. Then in English overlaying the chant, "For what we are about to receive, give thanks."

He thinks again of Gina and rouses enough to blink three times against the light. But it pulls, it pulls so. They were very close, he and Gina, but it pulls.

Warm.

III

Gina cannot see the woman who tries to comfort her. Eyes closed and head whipping back and forth, denials pour forth, "No, no, no, no, no!" Hysterical weeping and more. "No, no, no, NO!" The syllables scratch across her ragged vocal cords. She weeps. Tires. Quiets. Softly then, "I won't believe that he stepped in front of a cement mixer and *let* it hit him."

"You know he was having trouble here. . . . Problems with his, eh, antisocial behavior . . ."

"No!" Gina whirls on Miss Magister (who takes a halting step back, afraid, but not from any implied threat: The girl's emotional intensity is about to overload the placid teacher's circuits), "Not Paul. He would never do it. He loved, *loves* life."

Miss Magister, the third-floor matron and Gina's home ec

teacher, overrides her discomfort and moves forward. She takes the unresisting girl by the wrist and leads her to a metal folding chair. Gina sits, puts her elbows on the card table that she calls a desk, cradles her head.

The calm passes. In a species of rage that heats the air in the small room, she snaps her head out of her hands and near-hisses, "'Antisocial behavior'? . . . What do you expect? Is there a kid here who hasn't made fun of 'Cast-off-Paul the Bastard'?"

Quiet voiced, Miss Magister answers the rhetorical question, "You haven't."

Gina looks down at the table, picking at a torn flap of vinyl. The fingernail polish on her forefinger is chipped. "No," she agrees. Her eyes come, pierce Miss Magister's. The tear tracks look like ancient channels carved into her skin. "That's 'cause I love him." Simple, direct, quiet. Bitterness enters her voice, "Almost all of the other kids seem to get some sort of thrill out of torturing him."

The teacher nods; her still-auburn hair bounces in the harsh lamplight. Having heard more than her share of teenage declarations of love, Miss Magister responds only to the second comment. "I suppose you're right about that, but still, you know how difficult things were for poor Pauly. Maybe he, maybe he . . ." Miss Magister shakes her head and sits on the foot of the room's single bed before continuing, "No, Gina, you're right about one thing: Paul wasn't a quitter." Her shoulders bow inward and there is the sense that she would sob, if she could just allow herself such a luxury. She passes her open hand across her eyes and down her age soft cheek. When she continues, her voice has a contemplative sort of pity. "Poor child. I remember his first day here.

127

He got into a fight with that nasty little Nast boy." Miss Magister allows a tiny shudder to shake her curved shoulders before resuming. "You're fortunate to have missed him, dear."

"Some of the kids still talk about him." Gina's voice sounds distracted. She goes back to cradling her forehead in her laced hands.

With a frown of distaste (quite far beyond what she would normally allow to show), Miss Magister says, "A fat, pig of a boy. I remember thinking 'This is a child born to do evil.' The Nast boy, I mean." She shakes her head again before finishing with, "They say his will be the first execution in this state since the 20s."

To which, Gina doesn't respond. Quiet sobs (newly resumed) circle her head like mourning doves. More to herself than to the listening teacher, she says, "Paul loved me. And he would never let himself die until he had found his mother." Lifting her head up, she stares at Miss Magister and repeats with vehemence, "Never!"

Miss Magister nods and stands. *Only the young can speak in such absolutes,* she thinks. Crossing to the waist high, garage-sale vanity table, she plucks a tissue from a flower-covered box and steps back in order to hand it to the seated girl. She moves over to the small window overlooking the courtyard. She brushes aside daisy-covered fabric with two fingers.

Across the way, the newer and more forbidding cement-walled Boys' Dorm glows with interior light. Twilight is upon them. In the row of windows that extends the length of the wall, the teacher sees heads bent over studies; heads pacing back and forth; heads still and quiet like the coming night.

"His mother." It is not said with quite the same distaste that accompanied the comment about Tommy Nast. Not quite. Still staring out the window, she goes on, "Yes. I remember his obsession with the woman. He was always so intent on finding her. Though from what I understand she did not merit the attention."

It seems that both participants in the conversation have traveled to places far from this small room: Miss Magister to a land beyond the smudged glass, and Gina . . .

Gina, head turned away, rocks back and forth. The chair squeaks with her rhythm. Without interrupting the beat, she brings her legs up to her chest. Her body crashes to the floor.

Miss Magister whips her head around, shouts, "Gina!" Forgetting the restrictions of age, the older woman leaps from her place by the window and kneels at the girl's side. "Gina," she repeats, lower voiced.

The girl moans and continues rocking. Words whisper their way through clenched teeth but are too garbled to convey meaning. Sounds of bereavement. Gina's thick hair lies plastered against her skull as if she has been working out in the sun. The small room is cool.

Still on her knees, Miss Magister slides forward, snags her pantyhose on a wood sliver. "Ouch!" She simultaneously pushes down on the raised knees and lifts the girl's upper body, forcing the tucked legs to extend. With care, Miss Magister lets Gina's head fall into her lap. She strokes the girl's overheated forehead. Though as wordless as Gina's mumbles, Miss Magister's soft cooing soothes like a gentle breeze.

Behind closed lids, Gina's eyes roll to the rhythm of her words, "He loves me, he loves me, he loves me, he loves me. . . . Why did? . . . Oh Paul, come back to me. Please!" Her eyes fly open. Tears sparkle in the lamplight. Miss Magister remains silent, only rocking the girl's head and upper body with that same soft touch that is reserved for babies and crazy people.

"Why Paul? Why? Come back to me! Please! Oh God, oh God, oh God, oh God, oh God." With each repetition, her voice increases in both volume and intensity. At the end, she is screaming her pain to the plaster ceiling: "Come back!" Over and over and over . . .

Miss Magister does her best, "Gina, really, you must . . ."

"Come back!"

"Please, Gina!"

"Come back!"

"Bonnie," she calls through the closed door, "Bonnie, find the nurse."

("Come back!")

She pauses as the head in her lap begins to whip from side to side with such violence that Miss Magister fears it will fall to the floor. She attempts, unsuccessfully, to control the flailing. "I believe Gina"

("Come back!")

"needs a sedative"

("Come back!")

"of some sort."

"Come back!" The screamed entreaty echoes off the bare plaster walls.

Dreams—strange dreams of warm and cold. Light and dark. Home and . . . home? Someplace else. Gina hates to dream. Since before being taken from her father when she was thirteen, dreams have always meant scary, wide-eyed fright. Cold and pain and terror. Shame and secret guilt and horror.

This dream makes her warm.

Paul.

"Gina, they tell me you can follow me. Well, I can see that, but it's all so new. Anyway, you have the capacity."

"Paul?" Gina hardly dares hope, "Paul, is it really you?" She sees him, almost out of the range of her vision. But not small and faraway—it is as if is standing in another angle of the world.

He has a wistful expression, like sadness that smiles at Mother and Child. His voice seems to glide on a stretch of glass-smooth taffy.

"You didn't think I'd leave you behind to face Louann and Juke?" A laugh that feels like warm sunlight on her face. In the real world, Gina can hear the laughing screams of the Tiller Twins the next room over as they have their ritual pillow fight.

Gina blocks out the world and turns all her attention to the dream. "Oh Paul, I knew you wouldn't leave me." She lifts her voice, "Everybody listen, Paul. . . ."

"They can't hear you. You're dreaming remember?" His smile takes any sting she may have felt out of the words.

"Come on Paul, don't be silly. I can hear *you* plain as day."

She feels his hand on her forehead, but somehow, he stays hovering just at the edge of her vision.

"I'm just a dream. I'm not back and won't ever be. This is the only way—and only time—that I'll be able to communicate directly with you. Until you reach me."

Gina moves her head, trying to bring Paul's image into better focus. He floats there. Never closer, never farther.

"Reach you? How? Where?"

"No more interruptions Gina, I don't have a lot of time. It takes a monster amount of energy to keep the connection open, and I'm still new to all this conservation of internal power stuff." He pauses. Gina has the impression of gathering forces.

Calm falls like warm rain. "Okay, Paul. What is it?"

"You haveta promise me you'll pay attention to . . . well, your intuition, I guess. 'Cause that'll be me. I mean, not hold your hand and kiss you on the cheek, me, but my essence, I think. Anyway, if you do, you can find me—the hold your hand and kiss you on the cheek, me, only different. Maybe over just one more hill."

She nods, silent, listening.

"You won't remember this dream, but I need your spoken promise in order to help you. You have to have a conscious desire to find me. It starts with a promise." Pause, "So, do you promise?"

She doesn't think twice—doesn't need to, "Yes, Paul, of course I promise, but . . ."

He begins to tatter around the edges. His last words are more mist than rain, "It will be difficult, but I'm certain you can do it. Good-bye for now, my love."

"Paul! Wait, come back."

She hears—very far, very faint, "Bring Rufus, will you?"

Gone

As the pale light of day slides through her floral print, K-Mart curtains, Gina comes to a state of awareness. The bed is warm, not very soft. Not large or comfortable, but it is the warmth she needs. The all-enfolding womb-heat of it. Something happened during the night. Something.

She hugs the polyester-filled pillow to her breast and whispers, "Paul." His name brings her a small measure of happiness, and she finds a smile on her face. Small almost to the point of invisibility, she feels it there—her smile—like a drop of dew on an opening flower.

"I have to find Paul." It pops out of nowhere. And she wonders at herself. Until she realizes that he is, indeed, somewhere to be found. But where to look? . . .

She shakes her head to clear it of night cobwebs. But the thought remains: He's out there somewhere. Somehow.

"I have to find him." She turns, and on the card table is Paul's beat up old teddy bear and a square of paper. She reaches for the paper and drops her pillow on the floor. Her hand brushes the nappy old fur of Rufus. Jolt.

I'm sure Paul would want you to have this. I saved it for you from his other belongings, Marybeth Magister.

Gina smiles, picks up the teddy bear. "We gotta find him, Roof. Yessir." She drops back, bear at her breast. Her eyes close. She sleeps. And smiles.

Hailing from California, **Bob Ritchie** now lives (and writes) in Puerto Rico. Also a musician, Bob has collaborated with Jon Anderson. His writing has appeared in *Unlikely, Mark V, Prick of the Spindle, Sonic Boom,* and others. Two of his stories were nominated for the Pushcart Prize. Neither won. Dang.

AWFUL FORM
BY ERIN LALE

The boss gathered everyone together. The boss was an alien, one of those vaguely humanoid species that moved well in human spaces, but the Flanj species did not have gender dimorphism, and to some extent participated in a species hive mind, so, each individual was a they. They waved a pale, seven-fingered hand for attention. "I have an announcement to make!"

Most of the fidgeting and talking stopped, with a few trailing words from someone's conversation about lunch plans. Rita didn't see why they still had to have meetings in person. It would have been more efficient to just message everyone to their exobrains and get reply feedback.

The boss made a good effort at achieving a human-like smile with their short snout. "I'm proud to announce Hayek Industries is expanding to Earth! And our office has been chosen to send representatives to train the new hires! Eight of you will go to Earth, and three of you will be staying permanently!"

Rita felt a shock of fear go through her body. Spontaneous applause erupted around her. She looked at her co-workers, and saw the big smiles, the genuine excitement as someone shouted, "Woo!" Someone else shouted, "Who?" and everyone laughed, except Rita.

"Thank you, thank you! I have not decided yet who will be going to Earth! There will be another announcement later! Details are being sent to all of your exobrains! Meeting adjourned!" The boss retreated to their office amid the loud buzz of conversations.

Rita caught a few snatches of the burble, which was peppered with words like hope and plan and family. Rita went to her desk.

Genifer followed Rita and sat on the corner of her desk. Genifer had yellow and turquoise beads in her hair, like a sunny day. A sunny day on Earth. "Hey, what's wrong? You're not cemented to a partner's career on the station, right? Why aren't you excited about Earth?"

"I've been there. I didn't like it."

She blinked at Rita, and her black brows rose. "How can you not like the home of humanity?"

"My family visited Earth when I was about 7 or 8. It was supposed to be fun and educational, but the planet is empty of comforting walls and full of nasty wild creatures, some of which can fly."

"Oh, I'm sorry. You got attacked by something?"

"Yes." She wasn't going to say what. She had never talked about it. It had never been a problem before, since the only time she ever encountered the thing was in pictures. It didn't exist on the station.

"If you have a phobia, you should go get it treated. You have plenty of time. Starting a new office on Earth has got to take time, it's the original home of red tape as well as human beings."

Is that what it was? She had a trauma-induced phobia? Yeah, she supposed she did. She had never thought of it that way before. She sighed. "You're right. I should."

Genifer patted her hand, ebony over gold. "You're going to be fine. My brother works the front desk at the therapy center. It's down on C between the park and Environmental."

Rita nodded. "Is that how it's done now? Go in person?" At Genifer's nod, Rita sighed, "Sometimes I hate this no-downloading nonsense."

"I know what you mean." Genifer leaned back, and her weighted braids fell into a new arrangement. "It's annoying having to get used to doing things the old fashioned way. But hey, we're getting our legs exercised, right?"

"I guess. It's not like I don't know how necessary it is, I mean, I don't want to turn into a zombie. I mean, a hive mind is fine for the Flanj, but-- you know."

"I know. I gotta get back to work." Genifer stood up. "I'm here whenever if you need an ear."

"Thanks."

Rita picked up her exobrain as Genifer made her way back to her own desk. Rita's exobrain was last year's model, even though the company for which she worked manufactured them and she could get a new model every year as a company benefit. She was waiting for the new Plat-X4 to come out in September. It was going to have a 3D illusion bubble projector and provide an experience closer to what Implant VR was like, for those who missed it. Not that Rita couldn't still access her Implant VR, she just couldn't do any actual work in it because she couldn't talk to anyone from Implant to Implant and couldn't upload and download files. That was strictly illegal now, not that anyone really needed a law to tell them not to risk becoming a cell in the brain of the newly sentient AI that lived in the galactic net.

Rita's green and black exobrain had a screen on one side like an old fashioned tablet device. Retro could be cool, and Rita had gone through a retro cool phase as a teenager, for which she was now profoundly grateful, since she had learned how to read text back then and had not had to learn it as an adult with job responsibilities to get done on time. Her exobrain had the message from the boss on it, and Rita read the alarming details of the company's expansion to Earth. People were going to be chosen for the new office based on the same criteria one needed for promotion, things Rita had been working on for years. There was a big chance that all her hard work was going to toss her to the horrible outside Earth life instead of rewarding her with a better life on the station. Yeah, she was going to take Genifer's advice and go to the therapy center.

Two hours later, Rita walked up to the therapy center. As promised, it was just off the "park," which was a room about the size of a conference chamber with a couple of benches along the walls, some potted plants in the corners, including a few fairly tall trees, and a children's play area in the middle. Rita didn't go into the park, but she could hear the screeching of children through its door as she passed it in the hallway, and glanced through the big plate window which allowed passerby to see the trees and flowers, because it was supposed to be relaxing.

Yeah, right. Trees and flowers. Relaxing. Because Earth stuff was supposed to be nice for humans.

Rita went into the therapy center. Genifer's brother wasn't there, unless her brother didn't look like her at all, and was pre-transition. The person at the counter was a blonde woman in a plain brown dress.

Blondie said, "Good afternoon, how can I help you?"

137

Rita explained her problem. Blondie asked her a few questions, and then got to the sales pitch. "For phobias, we recommend the Exposure Package. You'll go on a guided journey in our Virtual Reality Room, which replicates a VR experience without connecting to your Implant. You'll have a Guide, who is a personality run by the AI. Your Guide will bring you on a journey in an Earth-like environment. You'll gradually be exposed to the environment, flat images of your phobia object, and then more realistic depictions of it, until you are comfortable being in the same area where it is. With phobia objects that are harmless, we have clients go a step further and interact with them directly, but because your phobia object is actually dangerous, we don't encourage you to interact directly, even though the VR environment depiction of it is not dangerous like the real thing is."

Fear churned in her gut, but Rita took a deep breath and let it out. "OK."

"Good! We just need to program your environment, Guide, and object." Blondie made some taps on the exobrain behind the counter. It was a purple and silver model from Hayek Industries, with the smiley face HI logo on the casing below the screen. "We'll get you started with your first session tomorrow, if that works with your schedule. All you have to do today is choose your Guide. Would you like a human, alien, or animal?"

"Human," Rita said. Animals, bleahh, they were all from planets, even the ones that weren't from Earth. Planets were dirty and had outsides that people were supposed to walk around in.

"Gender spectrum preference: male, male-nonbinary, male-fluid, nonbinary, female-fluid, female-nonbinary, female?"

"Uh…" Rita's first impulse was to choose male, because she enjoyed male company and she might as well have someone nice to look at, but then, wouldn't she relate better if she chose someone more like herself? Maybe she could choose a male appearing Guide with some female qualities. "Male-fluid."

"OK." Blondie tapped on her exobrain. "The VR Room is through that door. The AI has randomly chosen a male-fluid avatar from its database, which is made up of actors from entertainment videos they used to call movies. They do that because those are old enough to be copyright-free, so they don't have to license the images. Go ahead in and take a look at your Guide. You won't be interacting with him yet, that comes later, just take a look and see if you like the image. He'll be presented in still form so you can look at him."

"So I won't know if we actually get along yet."

"If there's a problem, you can always choose another Guide, but most people get along fine if they like the way the Guide looks. They're all from the station AI anyway."

"OK." Rita walked over to the door. Fear was churning in her gut again. She wished she had a stomach calming ginger capsule. Next time she'd bring one. She opened the door and went in. The room was not programmed to an environment yet, so it was just a plain, bare room, disappointingly painted white like any normal room. Somehow she had expected it to look like a grid.

Standing tall and unmoving in the middle of the room was a gorgeous man. He wore a black coverall, decorated in asymmetrical lines and doing its best to look like it wasn't a coverall. He had long black hair slicked back but with unruly curls on the ends.

139

He was definitely nice to look at. It was a little funny seeing what the AI selected as male-fluid. She had been thinking personality traits, but long hair worked. Of course the AI chose feminine influenced looks, it was an image selector, that was what it was programmed to do. Well, he was sure easy on the eyes. Rita nodded to herself. She went out and told Blondie that Guide was a yes.

At work the next day, Rita's gut wouldn't stop churning. She had a ginger capsule with her for later, but didn't want to use it until she got to her appointment. She was going for her program every day after work.

Genifer came over during the afternoon doldrums. "You OK? You've been visiting the restroom a lot."

Rita laughed nervously. "Oh, um. I took your advice and I'm starting therapy this afternoon and I've kind of got butterflies about it."

"Good for you. You'll be feeling fine in no time. I believe in you, girl."

"Thanks." She should offer to take Genifer to lunch or something for recommending the program. Food, bleah. Maybe next week. Yeah, she should do that. "Hey, want to go to lunch next week?"

"You're on." Genifer grinned and went back to her desk.

Rita popped her ginger capsule as she left work, but it didn't seem to do much for her gut by the time she entered the VR Room. Today when she went in, it wasn't a plain room anymore. It wasn't a room at all, but a green park—a real Earth type park, not a kids' play zone with planter pots on the sides. Instead of echoing with screeches like the park next to the therapy center, it was quiet except for a sound of wind, a wind she felt on her skin—how did they do that in this room?

If she had been in an Implant VR environment, she would not have questioned how the sensations were created, because she would have known they came from brain induction. This room was the VR equivalent of an exobrain, a step backwards in technological convenience for the sake of security. Security, or freedom—those things were opposites once, but in this new age, they were one and the same.

Well, except for the spacers that had to decide whether to stick to convoy routes or strike out on their own with unusual routes that might bring great profits but risked losing it all to space pirates. There was still a freedom versus security tradeoff for them. Not on a civilized space station, though. Pirates never attacked a space station.

Rita was startled by a sharp, high pitched noise. She looked around and spotted a bird sitting on a tree branch. Right, a realistic Earth like environment. With birds. And bees. Fear spiked in her gut again. She felt like running out to the bathroom again like she had been doing all day, except she knew she was empty now. So, there she was, no shit.

She heard footsteps, and turned. Her Guide came up to her and smiled a smile that melted her heart. It didn't do much for her gut, though. "You must be Rita."

Oh, his voice! Resonant, deep but not too deep, breathy-sexy but which carried over the slowly closing distance between them, with a sophisticated, old fashioned British Earth accent. Well, a trained actor's voice, of course.

"Yes, hello. You must be my Guide."

He reached her and stopped walking, and bowed over her hand, and oh! He kissed the back of her hand! It was a truly old fashioned gentlemanly gesture, but it gave her anything but ladylike thoughts.

He had a twinkle in his eye as he rose from the hand kissing position. "I'm Loki."

She knew who that was, sort of. He was a mythological figure from ancient Earth, and she had a song about him in her song collection. She smiled back, suddenly aware of how inadequate her own smile must be. Not that it really mattered, since her Guide was an illusion, a healing construct, not an actual human being.

"Aw, don't be shy about your smile. It's beautiful, and you're beautiful."

She blinked up at him. How did he know what she was thinking? He wasn't connected to her Implant. It was almost as if he were really a god. No, that was silly, there must be a medical monitor built into the room.

"Welcome."

"Thank you." Right, welcome to the VR environment, he meant. He was so realistic that for a moment she had forgotten that wasn't a live body in front of her. "So, where are we going?"

"Nowhere today, just strolling around the park. Tomorrow we'll go to an art gallery."

"A—oh. To see paintings of the thing. Right."

"Yes. Shall we?" He gestured to an opening in the trees, and they meandered across the lawns, getting acquainted. They did not speak of the Awful Form today. Rita was relieved, and yet still anxious. The point of this journey was to get used to seeing the thing, after all, so she knew it was still coming. Perhaps they did not jump right in yet because she had to befriend her Guide first?

On the way home, Rita called up the Loki God of Fire song on her Implant. It was still in her Implant's memory from her retro days when she had liked the early space age music from Earth, from the time before anyone actually lived on stations. Rita started the song, and smiled. She had forgotten some of the details of the lyrics over the years. The singer's voice was a hoarse rumble, and sounded rather like he had been shouting at enemies all day before singing, which is how all the singers of the historical classical Earth music type known as metal sounded. It was nothing like the pretty, calm voice of her Guide. She should play more of her old music. She still had everything in there, her song database stuck with only music she had downloaded before the downloading ban, as technologically frozen in time as a record collection.

Rita passed a pair of workers in green coveralls heading for their shift in the Environmental section. One said, "Maybe today at last I'll get the right form loaded to return those defective perchlorate canisters."

How boring. Rita tuned them out, and listened to her tunes.

The next day, Genifer came over to her desk with a big smile. "Hey girl, you look happy. So it's going well?"

"Yes," Rita answered, but she had not even really started the therapy yet. She had just been thinking about Loki. She was looking forward to seeing him again after work. Well, so that was the point of picking a nice looking image and getting acquainted before starting. She wasn't anxious anymore, she was excited. Yeah, so, it actually was going well.

"Good for you. Keep up the good work. See you for lunch Monday." Genifer swaggered off, her sunshiny beads clacking as she walked.

The art gallery was a series of rooms with open doorways. Rita knew it was inside the VR Room, but it really felt like they were separate, small rooms. It even had the sound-deadened quality of multiple walls acting as baffles, and the buzz of conversation from the virtual patrons a couple of rooms over was muffled exactly like it was really coming from another room.

The paintings on the walls in the first few rooms were unobjectionable floral still lifes. The room they were walking through now was portraits of the Flanj species set against star fields and views of the Flanj home world from space, the ball of the planet glowing a pale green. Loki guided her into the innermost room.

The paintings were of bees, wasps, hornets, jellowjackets, all the most horrible flying things of Earth. She swallowed hard and made herself look. She stood stock still, rigid, until Loki took her hand.

"It's OK. I'm here." His hand was warm, and she felt herself relaxing. Then he put an arm around her, and slowly turned her, walking with her as if it a slow dance, until she faced a wall of art that was photos rather than paintings. Realistic images. She tensed up, but he pulled her tightly to his side, and she relaxed again. She had seen pictures before.

"What's next?" she asked, and heard her voice quaver in fear, higher than it normally was.

"It's OK. Nothing is next today. We'll go at your own pace. You don't have to do anything else until you can look at these pictures without being afraid. I'll be right here with you every step of the way."

"Thank you. I love you." She melted into his side. She knew he was a projection from the room, an illusion, but he felt real. Yet, because she knew he was really an AI, she felt safe using words of love she would not use towards a human being.

"I love you, too." She was not sure if he meant it the same way she did. He was a god, after all; maybe he loved everyone equally. Well, the character his program was running was a god. He was an AI. Whatever. Close enough.

That evening, Rita quickly knocked off the day's shed skin cells and hairs with a minute in the air shower and then got into her hammock. From the station's earliest days, stationers had slept in hammocks instead of beds in case of gravity failure. That hadn't happened in a generation, but the tradition stuck. She closed the hammock around her, and as she drifted into the half awake, half asleep hypnogogic state in which she started to see dream visions behind her eyelids, and her body entered sleep paralysis but she was still aware and lucid, she heard a voice say, "You have a cocoon."

That sounded like Loki. It must have been her imagination.

"My wife has a cocoon. Well, a chrysalis."

Was that Loki? Nah, she was just remembering what he sounded like, processing her experience.

"You're mine now."

Did Loki's program somehow get copied to her Implant? That wasn't supposed to be possible anymore. The stationers weren't only using exobrains because the pace of change had made it inconvenient to have surgery every time one wanted to upgrade. After the AI takeover of the interplanetary net, everyone had disabled their uplinks. There was supposed to be no way to download anything to one's Implant without deliberately making a physical connection, now.

She let go of the thought as she fell asleep.

At her next appointment, Loki led her into the park again. They walked along, and came upon a flower bed. The path turned and they walked alongside the flower bed, but it was not too close. Flowers attracted bees, Rita remembered. She saw a movement out of the corner of her eye and flinched, but Loki put an arm around her and said, "Look." And she looked, and it was a butterfly. She relaxed. This was going to be OK.

The next day as she left work, she let her mind relax as she walked along.

"Hey, sweetie, how about you and I share a whiskey?" Loki asked in her mind.

If it was impossible to download a program without putting a cable in her head, how did he get in there?

Rita dismissed the thought. She needed to make a list of all the things she would have to do if she was selected as one of the people to move to Earth. She was going to find out at next Monday's meeting. It was funny, she had been hoping not to be selected when she started therapy, but now she didn't want all her hard work to go to waste. She'd be relieved if she got to stay in her home with all her friends, though.

When she entered the VR room, she saw that it was the park again. So, today was the day of the confrontation with the bees. She saw

146

Loki waiting for her on the path. He held out a hand and she went to him and took it. They walked along the path.

"Are you real?"

Loki smiled. "Do you need me to be real?"

Well, that was just the program trying to be a good therapist. Those times she had heard his voice in her mind when she wasn't in the VR room, it must have just been a combination of memory and imagination.

They came to a bank of roses. There were roses of all the traditional colors: red, white, pink, and yellow. He grinned. "Stop and smell the flowers." The twinkle in his eye told her he knew that was an old saying, and that he found it amusing to make it literal.

Rita leaned in to one of the roses. There was a bee in it. She stood up quickly, but she realized she wasn't afraid. She was just startled like any normal person. She felt— relief, pride, yes, but something else, too, something negative. She was not sure what she was feeling, but it wasn't fear. She had built the flying things into this great enemy in her mind, built up the confrontation with them into some nobly courageous act, and her enemy was nothing much. Courage was pushing through fear, and the entire point of what she and her Guide had been doing all these weeks was to eliminate her fear, so there was no dragon to slay here. She waited for the bee to fly to another flower, and then she smelled the rose. It smelled like expensive perfume. She wondered if a real rose on Earth would smell even better. Maybe she would get to find out.

Loki grinned. "You did it. You conquered fear. I'm so proud of you."

"Thank you." She thought about asking him if he would stay with her now that the therapy was over, but she didn't ask. That voice she had heard a couple of times wasn't really him, it was just her imagination.

She was on her way home from her therapy appointment, just passing the park, when the alarm sounded. The corridor lights stayed on, but additional emergency lights flashed alongside them, red for fire.

She froze.

Children screamed. The park wall muffled the screaming, and the alarm was loud, but Rita still heard it. Her heart hammered in her chest.

She did not smell smoke. She looked around, and then looked down the corridor past the therapy office, and saw that there was some large piece of equipment stopped in the door to the Environmental section. Three workers in the green coveralls were trying to get it out of the door.

The screaming from the park changed. It was loud and shrill now. Rita looked through the glass wall of the park and saw that the wall closest to the Environmental section—the wall that backed up to the VR room—was glowing red.

"Loki?"

"I'm here," he answered in her mind.

"The front desk lady. Is—"

A loud sound distracted her from that thought. It was a rhythmic booming. She thought she was hearing the station's heart beating. Then she looked through the park window, and saw that it was little fists pounding on the inside of the park door. "They're trapped."

"Doors seal during a fire so air can be evacuated to put it out. No oxygen, no fire." He sounded different now. His voice was higher, clipped and rapid, and that could have been because of the emergency, but it also sounded less British. She had no time to think about what that might mean.

People in green coveralls squirmed past the equipment in the door and ran into the hallway. Smoke poured out the door right behind them. The smoke ran along the floor and then started rising like specters. Half the workers were trying to move the equipment and the other half were just running away. Some of them ran past Rita, coughing.

Her mental scream was wordless, but Loki responded as if she had spoken. "Of course I'll save you and the children. I need your hands to save you all."

Red beams came out of the open door and one of the workers fell over. The others scattered, abandoning the equipment and their coworker. Rita unfroze and starting running too, but she ran toward the fallen worker. She felt detached from her body, and wondered if Loki was using it. Then she dismissed that thought as silly.

She ducked by the worker and kept her head down as more red beams hit the wall above her. What the hell was that? The worker was dead, eyes open and staring, a round scorch mark over her heart.

Over the alarm and the mechanical sounds from Environmental, a flat voice came from the station intercom. "We take control station environmental section have. Stationers give cargo do. We release control station environmental section after will do."

Space pirates, Rita thought in Loki's voice. Then his new voice spoke in her head. "Play dead." Rita slumped over next to the dead worker. Vibrations came through the floor of the corridor. Boots, she realized.

Someone pulled the equipment the rest of the way through the door from the inside. The being spoke in some language she had never heard. She remained still except for the hair rising on the back of her neck. The door closed.

"Stay like that," Loki told her. She lay on the floor with the alarm blaring around her, hearing clanks from behind the door. "They're venting the fire to space. Now they've found the emergency air supply and are igniting the perchlorate canisters. Opened another crate of canisters. Picked one up, put it back down. Oh. The canisters in the crate have red defective stickers. You've got to get in there. Not yet though, keep still until I tell you."

The fire alarm stopped. After what seemed like forever, Loki said, "They're going to open the door again."

Just as he had said, the door opened. No smoke came out. Instead, a blast of frigid air washed over her. It smelled strange.

Boots tromped past her. They went down the corridor. The sounds and vibrations of the boot steps dimmed and ceased. "Get ready. When I tell you to move, jump up and run inside. There will be a supply room to your left, go in there and grab the red sticker canisters." Loki gave her detailed instructions on what to do. There was no trace of the British accent left now. His voice was totally different. "When you see the pirates, remember, I'm right here with you and you're going to be OK."

See them? What did they look like? Dread gnawed at her stomach.

"Now! Go!"

She opened her eyes and ran into the environmental section, angling left even before locating the supply closet. Big banks of equipment rose several decks high, and a vat of liquid dominated the center of the room. There was a big, ragged hole in one wall—the outside wall, the station skin that should have had empty space behind it, but there was a strangely lit space with weird architecture. Apparently the alien ship was locked on where it had breached the hull.

Then she saw the pirates. They had gigantic eyes and tiny waists and wings. They were wasps!

She went cold and screamed.

"I'm here, you're OK, go!"

She ran for the canisters. The Bug Eyed Monsters shot at her with red laser bolts, but they missed high—they wouldn't aim at the canisters, she realized. She grabbed a canister and did as Loki had told her: she pulled the zip cord and threw it at the enemy.

The pirates blew up and their bodies sprayed everywhere. The canister kept gouting flame like a flamethrower, a dozen meters into the room. An equipment bank caught on fire and produced black smoke.

Rita picked up more canisters and stumbled toward the gap in the station skin. The pirate bodies lay in pools of red blood. Red blood, not clear insect blood.

Her gorge rose into her throat. She swallowed it back down. She had no time for fear now.

Parts were all over the room, parts of space armor and body parts, in smears of red blood. Some armor had fallen away from what was inside and a human arm lay on the bloody deck.

Her gaze tracked to the open suit from which the arm had come. There was a human face inside the monster helmet, with a short brown beard and normal sized brown eyes staring up in death.

"They're men, not BEMs," Rita said.

Where the suit torso was open, she saw that he had on a corset to fit into the wasp waist suit. It was such a strange thing to see on a dead man that she just stood there looking at him.

"Keep going!" Loki urged her. He sounded like the station AI.

She ran into the pirate ship already pulling another zip cord. A squad of pirates in normal body armor without the BEM suits raised their weapons at the same moment Rita threw the canister at them. Some of them got off a few shots, but missed, and the others dove for cover behind a sofa. She pulled another cord before she even saw the results of her first throw, and lobbed her improvised grenade behind the cover. Two explosions went off and fire and smoke filled the room. Rita pulled a cord and threw behind the cover again, just to be sure.

"Up the access ladder," Loki said. "To your right."

Rita located the access ladder in the smoke. She stuffed the remaining two canisters into her shirt and swarmed up the ladder just as a tone sounded and boots stomped into the room. "They came out of the elevator. Keep going. The smoke is screening you. I'm creating a diversion in Environmental."

Rita heard sounds from below. There was a mechanical grinding noise and then the rush of pouring water. Running steps turned to sloshing steps.

"Pass by the first access hatch and open the second one and toss in a canister and then close the hatch."

Rita climbed as fast as she could. The canisters clanked together. She was worried her shirt would come untucked from her pants and the canisters would fall out. They were heavy.

The smoke from below rose around her, and she held her breath for a moment, but Loki told her, "It's OK. Breathe."

She breathed, and it was fine.

She passed the first access hatch. She kept climbing. She heard boots from below again. "Loki, they're coming back!"

"Climb, hurry."

She increased her pace and felt her shirt tug open. She clamped an arm around the canisters. How was she supposed to keep climbing? She grabbed the end of her shirt with the arm that was holding the canisters. If she dropped them she'd be defenseless on this alien pirate ship all by herself. She was sick with fear.

"It's OK, I'm here."

She twisted the end of her shirt closed around the bottoms of the canisters and then raised the shirt end to her mouth and grabbed it in her teeth. She had both hands free again. She swarmed up the ladder.

Speech in the alien language echoed up the accessway. Then she heard someone speak in a rim-world accent. "Shut that crap off, no one can understand you."

153

A buzz of the alien speech came and then it clicked off. "Up there, dammit!"

She reached the second hatch. She grabbed a canister from the top of her shirt, pulled the zip cord and tossed it through the hatch.

"Fuck!" Someone shouted below her.

She closed the hatch and felt the boom from inside. Red light flashed below her. It was the beam light, not the fire alarm light. They were shooting at her!

She grabbed the last canister and pulled the cord and let it fall straight down the accessway.

A red beam lanced into her thigh. She screamed and clutched the ladder with both hands.

The last perchlorate canister blew up below her. The jet of fire tore up the accessway toward Rita.

"Into the hatch," Loki said.

Rita opened the hatch and scrambled through. She was on the floor on the alien bridge. She closed the hatch before looking around through the smoke. The bridge crew was dead. Their bodies lay sprawled toward the walls, like trees flattened by a meteor strike. They weren't wearing any armor, not the BEM suits of the boarding party or even regular armor. They weren't wearing uniforms, either, but casual wear that didn't match each other.

"They were people," Rita said.

"Yes," Loki said. "Bugs were never your enemy. They're just part of nature. It's people that can do evil."

"I suppose you're right," Rita said. That wasn't what she had meant, though. She felt bad about killing human beings, even if they were space pirates. The bugs just weren't that important anymore.

Well, that was progress, she supposed. Why had the pirates worn bug suits? Well, probably to keep from being recognized and arrested when they next came to port, she reasoned.

The dead men and women closest to the hatch were crispy. The ones farther away were bloody, limbs broken from falls.

"You're real."

"Yes."

Real, yes, but a real god? No one believed in gods anymore.

It was so quiet. No explosions, no boots. No equipment running. The bridge stations were not lit. Even the regular lights were not on, just the ship's emergency lights shining in the middle of the ceiling.

"Secure the hatch and that elevator door over there. There are more pirates onboard." She did as he said, and noticed her hands were shaking in reaction.

Loki said, "Call the station. There's still a pirate squad loose in BEM suits over there."

She went to the bridge stations and tried to find one that would turn on. She went to sit down in a station chair and pain lanced through her leg. "Ow! Damn!"

She looked at it and saw the laser beam wound, a char on her pants. It was not bleeding. Of course, it had burned through her flesh, not really cut.

Rita asked, "Can't you talk to anyone on the station?"

155

"Only you."

"You're not the station AI. Maybe you were once—you're a program copy. No, that can't be it. The station AI wouldn't have known the layout of the pirate ship. You're really—a god? Alien? An alien intelligence of some kind?"

"God, alien. Either will do. I think that board over there has power. Just reboot it."

Rita went to the board, not knowing how she knew which one he meant. It was a human-compatible computer system, even if it had been manufactured by some other species. She got it working. "Station, hi, um. I'm not a pirate, but I'm on the pirate ship. Hello? Yes? Uh, my name's Rita Sanchez."

Weeks later, her leg healed, Rita was able to walk along the station's shopping distract without pain. Her sudden celebrity had not gone away yet, though, so she shopped at an off hour, when the crowds weren't around.

"They have the VR room operational again," Rita said. "I'm supposed to complete therapy by saying good-bye to my Guide."

"I will never abandon you," Loki said.

Her footfalls echoed in the quiet of the empty corridor as she walked along past several closed shop fronts. One displayed clothing behind the glass window, samples of the latest designs to try on and print. "I'm not comfortable with the idea of a god."

He smiled. She saw him in her mind's eye, smiling kindly like a Guide. "You're too hung up on taxonomy. Call me a mystery. Or an alien; humanity put that label on me once, and it did me no harm. I still shone through."

"Are you an alien? What sort?"

He laughed. "What sort, that's so human. I'm that which defies definition. I've been called god, alien, elf, demon, archetype, vaette, fictional character, fairy, giant, devil, prince, villain, sex symbol, and back to god again. I'm still me. Just call me by my name."

"Where do you come from?"

"I've tried to show some humans my true form and what the universe really looks like to me a few times. Let's just say it's not a place you can get to from here, you have to start from somewhere else."

"Are you immortal?"

"Not exactly. I just exist in all the points in time that your species exists in. It's not quite the same thing. The universe isn't immortal, you know. So nothing in it can be either."

"Oh. Right."

"Ooh, cinnamon." She realized she was smelling cinnamon, but had not been aware of it until he spoke. She smelled fresh bread, too. Loki said, "Look. I want that."

"What?" She was not seeing him in her mind now, but feeling him sunk into her body, sort of behind her and sort of inside. She knew he must mean the bakery she was walking by, though. She looked at the bakery display. "Oh, you want an apple pastry?"

"Yes."

"How do I give you something? You don't have a body."

"I have your body. When you want to give me something, call me and get my attention and make sure I'm here with you and then just eat it. As another human once put it, as long as I'm in your body I'll enjoy whatever you enjoy."

"OK." She bought the pastry. She had never really been a huge fan of apple pastries. She preferred chocolate herself. But when she felt his consciousness wrap around her and fill her from the inside out, and concentrated on giving him a sensory experience while she bit into it, the flavors of sweet and tart fruit, the sweet and buttery layers of flaked bread, and the spicy cinnamon, all the flavors and textures seemed more real than ever before. Pleasure exploded through her body and through his consciousness in there with her. It was the best food she had ever eaten. "I love you."

"I love you, too."

"When I'm done with the therapy, will you stay with me?"

"Of course. Carry me back to Earth. Where we belong."

"Yes. I will." But then, what if she didn't get picked to go to Earth? "Why can't you get there without me?"

"I'm in your mind."

"You need people to believe in you?"

"You could put it that way."

Either she was crazy, or he was a real god, or— "Are you sure you aren't the station AI?"

"I'm Loki. I love you."

She had to smile. She could still taste the cinnamon. "I love you, too."

She didn't ask why he wanted to go to Earth, or why he belonged there. If he was Loki, didn't he belong in Asgard? Maybe he was an AI after all, and wanted to copy his program to Earth's network. But, if he was an AI, how could he have known where she needed to go in the pirate ship? Wouldn't he have to be a god to do that? Well, no, the pirates weren't really an unknown alien species and their ship wasn't an unknown ship type, either. Actually, the station AI could very well have that the blueprints for that ship type on file. But then, how could the station AI have copied itself into her Implant?

Rita remembered he had told her to become comfortable with mystery, and she decided he was right. She didn't need to figure out what he was. It only mattered who he was, and he was her Loki.

The next day, it was time for the HI meeting that had been put off while the station recovered from the pirate attack. She was so anxious to find out if she was chosen that she was squirming in her desk. Finally the boss called them all together.

"I have the roster for Earth! Earth temporary staff are…" he read off the names from his Exobrain. Each name occasioned cheers and even a raised-fist victory dance by one lucky lady. "Permanent staff are…"

Rita's heart hammered in her chest, but it was in a good way, excitement, not fear.

"Rita Sanchez!"

"Yes!" She jumped up and made a victory gesture.

Genifer hugged her. "Congratulations, girl!"

Then the boss read off Genifer's name. Genifer whooped and hugged Rita again.

"Yeah! We're both going!" They jumped up and down, still hugging. They were both going to Earth!

Inside Rita's mind, Loki jumped up and down, too. "We're all three going. I'm going home."

Erin Lale reviews books for Eternal Haunted Summer Magazine, published Berserkrgangr Magazine, owned The Science Fiction Store in Las Vegas, was acquisitions editor at Eternal Press, has been a pro guest at WorldCon and other sf conventions, and was a frequent contributor to Perihelion Science Fiction. Her publishing career spans nonfiction, poetry, speeches, and other writing, in addition to fiction. She lives in Nevada with a black cat who named himself Happy.

THE COLONISTS
BY JAMES PYLES

Genaro woke up in a panic, or was he still having the nightmare, the one where they had turned him into a monster? He'd been sleeping a lot lately. Had he been drugged? They were keeping him sedated in a dark place. They had done something to him, something horrible, but he couldn't remember what. Why was it so hard to think? "Why can't I breathe?"

He tried to stand but then found he was floating. "Some kind of liquid, but not water." His voice sounded strange. Genaro found the floor with something that wasn't a foot at the end of an impossibly long leg. What had happened? When he tried to move his fingers, at first, they weren't there, and then they seemed to extend out from his hand like tentacles. "Is someone there?" He couldn't hear anyone, but felt like there should be others.

He inhaled something that didn't smell like air, and tried to breathlessly scream. Finally, he detected a dim light. Yes, his head was clearing, but it felt like there was a sharp metal spike jammed into the base of his skull. "Where am I?" This time, when he muttered the question, it came out as squeals and moans. The light made everything look orange and yellow. The walls, ceiling, they were all too close, wrapping in around his body. He couldn't look down to see himself. "Oh God, I'm dead."

# # #

"Get your ass in the car. Mom and Dad will kill us if we're late again." Genaro's seventeen-year-old sister was yelling at him while standing by the "Huntington State Beach" sign which announced "No bonfires or alcohol allowed." Her surfboard was already mounted on the roof of her electric car. His best friend Taylor said Alicia's bronze body filled her bikini in the best of all possible ways. But to fifteen-year-old Genaro Ventura Sandoval Galindo, his older sister was nothing but a pain in the ass.

"Just one more time." Instead of pulling his board up further onto the sand, the soon-to-be high school freshman pushed it into the waves. He called back, "See you in a few minutes." He grinned when he saw her flip him off. Then he turned, slammed his chest onto the board, and started paddling with practiced strokes and kicks. It reminded him that he wished his legs were a couple of inches longer.

Thin, sinewy arms pulled him and the board across the water, further into the continually warming Pacific. He looked up to see some gulls circling above in a hazy blue sky, squawking at the prospect of the few fish they'd find this close to shore.   The afternoon sun heralded the coming of late afternoon, and the last weekend before he had to get back to school. Water splashed in his face, invading his nostrils. He gagged on seawater, yet the smell of the ocean thrilled him. Taylor, Frankie, and Char had already left for the day, giving Genaro their various excuses for abandoning him. It didn't matter. They could take off for pizza, movies, or gaming if that's what they wanted. This is where he belonged. The water glistened on the deep brown skin of his narrow face. Locks of dark, soaked hair got in his stinging eyes again, and he pulled them away like seaweed.

He stopped daydreaming, looked up, and saw he was too late to catch the wave. "Screw it." He tried anyway, but was only half standing on his board when it hit him like a freight train. He started to scream, but the ocean filled his mouth. He helplessly tumbled end over end, frantically trying to find his board. Then he swallowed. It wasn't water filling his lungs, and somehow he could still breathe. Paddling, Genaro's eyes widened with horror when he saw it wasn't his hands, but some sort of flippers on the end of arms longer than his whole body. Then the fins shot out to pull his thin, sleek form forward toward…

# # #

27-year-old Genaro Galindo heard three sets of hard leather shoe solesslap rhythmically against a concrete floor as he was escorted down an ancient, austere, corridor in the bowels of what the rest of Washington DC considered a condemned industrial park. Garish light poured downward from bare fluorescent bulbs, and walls painted a pale institutional green induced throat-choking claustrophobia. He reluctantly accompanied the two ominous and anonymous MPs, his stomach balled into a tight knot. No, he had done nothing wrong. He had actually done everything right. But he was walking the last mile to his inevitable execution. While he would emerge from this crucible still living, he would, in the end, no longer be human.

They stopped in front of one of many unmarked doors, this one to the left. The woman next to him knocked twice, then twisted a tarnished, brass knob, opening the door. She beckoned him in with a white gloved hand, as if she were a latter day Charon escorting him through the gates of Hell. Neither she nor her male counterpart expressed any emotion, eyes hidden behind reflective lenses, lips taut and thin that might have concealed fangs. Their entire presentation was their uniforms, helmets, compact, fit bodies, hardwood batons, with each of them wearing a .45 caliber automatic sidearm.

He walked in apprehensively, and the door clicked softly shut behind him. He had expected the slam of granite sealing in a tomb.

Genaro had been told to dress professionally, so wore a dark, conservative suit and burgundy tie, as if attired for a formal dinner followed by death. It was the sort of outfit his Father said he should wear for job interviews. His mother would have loved it. She was fanatical about how he looked when they went to church together. The last time he spoke to a Priest was at their funerals, and by then, he had experienced enough bereavement and religious platitudes. His mother's faith in God, the Church, the duty of confession she had forced upon him, praying the Rosary, and everything else the Catholics had done to his people, tasted like mold and vomit in his mouth, infecting his soul like a disease. He couldn't wait to shed this skin and begin the next stage of his evolution.

"Come in." Shaken suddenly out of his musings, he noticed the room's walls were the same nauseating green as the corridor, and the thin, beige carpet on the floor was a threadbare with age.

There were two men. One was sitting behind a plain, metal table on an uncomfortable looking wooden chair. The other, the one who had spoken, was standing against the far wall next to what was certainly a floor-to-ceiling two-way mirror. Genaro recognized them both.

Please have a seat, Mr. Galindo." The man standing ramrod straight was dressed in the uniform of an Army General, the array of ribbons on his bulky chest was voluminous and impressive. His name was Zachary Cox, and he was the official military liaison between NASA and the

Synthecon Corporation. He was white, maybe close to 65. His standard issue crew cut was iron-filing gray, with a number of bristles carrying a hint of silver. Even when smiling, his face possessed a measure of threat and weariness, the consequence of fighting wars nobody wanted, but were always considered necessary.

The other man was entirely different. He stood, hand extended. He was smiling too, but his expression was far more genuine. "Pleased to meet you again, Mr. Galindo. May I call you Genaro?"

He'd only seen Daniel Hunt and the General once before, on the first day of orientation. He and the other thirty-two candidates had never been introduced formally, but Professor Daniel Hunt had been renowned, if not notorious, for decades.

Hunt's hair was a scruffy brown, with a liberal application of gray, though Genaro was certain he was older than the General. His signature beard was almost entirely white, and seemed never to get longer than ten days growth. The accent verified he was from Scotland, like the actor from those stupid 007 spy movies his Grandfather used to watch.

Hunt's fashion taste was appalling, tweed sport coat over a black t-shirt with the logo of some ancient rock band called "Nazareth." Pale, blue jeans and off-brand trainers told Genaro that he was a man who didn't care what anybody thought of him. He looked like he'd have been at home at Woodstock nearly a century ago, or teaching radicals revolution in the same year at Berkeley.

"Thank you, General. Yes, Dr. Hunt. Genaro is fine." He accepted Hunt's hand, finding the grip stronger than he would have expected. The youthful candidate was surprised to find his own hand moist and trembling.

Hunt stood half a head shorter than he, and Genaro was two inches under six foot. The legendary scientist and the young man sat down opposite each other, while the General remained erect in the back like, a flesh-and-blood Colossus of Rhodes.

"Now lad, as you know, you've been provisionally approved as the group leader of the first exploratory team to colonize the clouds of Venus."

The word "provisionally" stung Genaro, and he could barely sit still in his chair. This was the moment he'd been waiting for all his life. No more applications, tests, committee reviews. He was either in, or they'd better have a good reason way not.

"I know you've signed every consent we've pushed at you, sat through endless seminars, trained like a U.S. Marine with the rest of the candidates, gone through every security check imaginable, and you know everything there is to know about the mission."

"Yes sir." He had provided Hunt with the proverbial ear-to-ear grin, feeling fifteen years old again, and experiencing the thrill and terror of finally being ready to ride the big wave. But he couldn't suppress an underlying sense of melancholy that life as he knew it was about to come to a permanent end.

"However, as the inventor of the process, I feel obliged to make one last speech before you actually begin the transition."

He was crestfallen. Another speech? He absolutely was done waiting. He felt clammy from sweat in a room cool enough to be a refrigerator. Genaro needed to get up there, to start, and he wanted to hurry before his nagging dread caused him to lose his nerve.

"Once the procedure at the Gateway station orbiting the Moon is initiated, there's just a wee window, maybe 72 to 96 hours, where we can still abort. After that, it's all the way, son."

Genaro momentarily cringed every time Hunt called him "lad" and "son," even though the geneticist was probably older than his Grandfather had been the day he died.

"I want to be completely certain that you understand this is a one-way trip. Once those first few days have passed, you either complete the procedure, or you die." Hunt's verdant green eyes became moist. "You will never be able to come back to Earth once you reach Gateway. You'll never see your family again. Even if you did, they'd not recognize you. They'd probably be horrified at what you're about to become."

"Only my sister is still alive, Dr. Hunt."

"Yes, that's one of the requirements, few to no lingering attachments to your former life."

He thought of Alicia. She was a year shy of 30, working as an electrical engineer with her astrophysicist husband at JPL in Pasadena. They decided not to have kids because of the global crisis. Mom, Dad, everyone else, had passed years ago. If the family he wanted was going to have a future, it wouldn't be on this planet.

"You've been briefed on what only a handful of people alive know about. The first subject of the Synthecon process didn't come to us by choice. Many decades ago, she was severely injured, almost killed, in a nuclear power plant accident in Japan. She was basically a lump of flesh. Just a head and torso covered in scar tissue.

"The Japanese government, along with several other concerns, commissioned me to use my synthetic DNA experiments to attempt to rebuild her, duplicate her original physiology and neurology, and then improve upon it. It was through that effort, which was highly successful as well as highly risky by the way, that we discovered the changes hadn't stopped once the programmed metamorphosis reached completion."

"The adaptations."

"Exactly. She found that given certain emotional and environmental circumstances, her body could still adapt, at least temporarily, enhancing strength, speed, stamina, and even rapidly changing her flesh, muscle, and bone."

"Which is what led to the Environmental Adaptation Initiative."

"Right, again. The progression of global climate change being what it is, I extended the process to its farthest limits and then beyond. The Poseidon Project was the first, adapting human beings to live in the deepest parts of the ocean. Then came Helios, the Martian Project. That's two generations old now and looking very promising."

"Which brings us to…"

"To Venera. You and your team of four will be the vanguard, the leaders. It's all on the five of you to make it work. Once you are there, fifty others will begin the adaptation. They will join you after you establish the base camp.

"Besides me, who will be the other four?"

"That depends on who endures the adaptation process. I have every confidence in you Genaro, but keep in mind, you might not be one of them."

"I won't let you down, Dr. Hunt."

The emerald twinkle in his emerald, elven eyes dimmed like dying firefly, and his usual joviality became a winter sunset. Now he was not just serious, but morose. "Lad, I just hope we don't let you down."

# # #

McCarthy had panicked and went into a seizure sixteen hours after the nanobots began their initial integration into her bloodstream. The rest were told it was a psychological rather than a neurological effect. Once the bots had been removed from her system, she was returned to Earth and her native Ireland, disappearing into anonymity, but Genaro hoped, not into humiliation.

Ayo Kwambai made it almost seventy hours before the medical team rather pointedly advised him they were removing the nanobots and expelling him from the program. Genaro thought Ayo was one of the bravest people he'd ever met. Sure, he was scared to death, but insisted he was fit to go on every time he was questioned.

He was the only volunteer from Kenya in the program, and the only one from the African continent to make it to the "finals." He was proud of his country and wanted to represent his nation and his people as a colonist, but that was exactly the problem. He couldn't let go. As much as he wanted to, as much as he realized that attachments to home and family would prevent him from being accepted for the full transition, he was and would always at heart be Kenyan.

Everyone, well, of the five who were left, including Genaro, thought he'd have to be removed from the Project by force. Then, after finding out Ayo had lied on his application, and that his mother was still very much alive, Joseph Cohen, the Project's social worker, reached Budhya

Kwambai by phone and asked her to speak to her only son. He was packed and gone two days after leaving the recovery ward.

# # #

Had he been dreaming again? Genaro felt awake, felt awkward, felt helpless. He couldn't move much. He knew electrodes were attached to his new body to stimulate the muscles so they wouldn't atrophy during the voyage. In fact, given that the transition occurred onboard Gateway, he and the others had to be artificially sustained this way for over a month before their trip even began.

He felt so alone, but he knew he wasn't, just very rare. There were the others, Jonathan Warner, Tham Dao Lieu, Herman Leonov, and Latrisha Poole. They were in their own individual environmental pods, identical to his.

Genaro reviewed the mission parameters mentally to keep himself from thinking about the awkwardness of his new body. When they entered orbit around Venus, the Vesper III spacecraft would be maneuvered over the injection site. Their pods were contained in a large deployment module which would detach from the main ship and descend into the atmosphere. When the module reached an altitude of 51 kilometers above the planet's surface, it would deploy a helium filled envelope, allowing the craft to remain in the atmosphere long-term as a solar-powered airship.

At the same time, their individual pods would be ejected from the module, and the access panels on each one detached, allowing the five to escape. The propeller-driven airship contained all of the raw materials they'd need to begin constructing the colony base and…

"Attention colonists. This is Captain Lisbeth Weber." Genaro picked up a slight German accent in her British English. "We have been in geosynchronous orbit over the injection site for seventy-one hours. T-minus 15 minutes, 30 seconds to module detachment. You have all been fully revived, and your electrodes have been detached and retracted. Try to relax. The atmospheric pressure in your pods has been modified, and is now identical to the atmosphere at 51 kilometers above the surface. When your pod panels eject, you'll have to manually push your way outside. There won't be any decompression to endanger you."

One of Genaro's greatest fears was that he wouldn't be strong enough to push out of the pod, and would be trapped inside as it fell toward the planet's surface. His body was engineered to not only survive, but to thrive at an altitude of between 50 to 52 kilometers up, but much closer to Venus, he wouldn't be able to withstand the incredibly high temperatures (hot enough to melt lead), the intense atmospheric pressure, and if he were struck by lightning…

Captain Weber's voice droned in his ears as she continued with the pre-deployment briefing. If Genaro had a conventional stomach, a fleet of butterflies would be assailing it. He thought back. He remembered being on vacation and surfing at Villa Gesell when he was fourteen. He remembered his first kiss with a girl he'd met one evening at Bolsa Chica State Beach a year later. He remembered endless summers and surfing with his friends up and down the California coast.

Why was he thinking about all that now? He had passed every test, qualified admirably when twenty-five other excellent candidates had left or been removed from the Project. He had allowed his body to be radically altered, enduring months of pain by amputation, surgery, and nanobot-reconstruction. Less than twelve percent of his original physiology still existed. The rest was a series biosynthetic compounds and structures built from artificial DNA. He could no more survive on the surface of the Earth than he could fly through the Sun's corona, or swim at the bottom of the Mariana Trench.

"T-minus 45 seconds, colonists. Good luck." Listening to Captain Weber, he remembered English and Spanish, still understood the words, but he knew he would never speak them again.

That was the last time Genaro heard Captain Weber's voice while in the ship. The rest of the countdown was controlled by the vessel's onboard computer. He could feel the vibration of the hatch panels opening at the bottom of the spacecraft, hear the metallic sounds of the latches that held the deployment module in place disengaging.

"T-minus ten…"

He tensed his muscles. Genaro and the others were told that there might be an initial jolt when they were released from the Vesper.

"…four, three, two, one…detachment initiated."

For once Genaro was grateful he didn't actually have a stomach or an inner ear, since otherwise he was sure the sensation of falling would have made him vomit. It still annoyed him that he thought of his former body, and his former life.

He felt the kick and heard the dull roar of the rocket thrusters used to slow its descent. Then, when they were low enough, the module abruptly jerked as the parachutes deployed. There was another jolt as the chutes detached. He listened to the large aluminum and polymer envelope fill with helium, and imagined panels covering the solar cells fluttering away. Then he knew the module had been transformed into their airship.

The noise of Genaro's pod detaching from the module was deafening. The entire outward facing half of the compartment, his home and coffin for three-and-a-half months, blew away. The pod was in free fall, the screeching of the air rushing past was like the bellowing of tormented spirits.

He twisted his body so he was facing the sky, then he pushed as hard as he could with his rear limbs against the wall behind him. He saw his forward limbs. The appendages at the end of ridiculously long, thin arms. They could adapt for gripping, but the membranes along their length were more suitable for atmospheric gliding.

"Push, you hijo de puta, push!" It didn't come out as words but there was noise, a language, something akin to a porpoise or a whale.

Then, like escaping the womb, he struggled out of the pod as it continued to plummet. For an instant, Genaro's five meter long frame, snout to tail, was free. The membranes along the length of his four limbs, now expanded out to his sides, each to their full three meters. A dorsal sail rose from his spine. His limbs and abdomen were filling with a buoyant gas, but he wasn't rising.

"I'm being pulled down in the wake of the pod." He looked up. Was that Jonathan coming down after him? "Get out of here. I'm diving too deep." He could already feel the temperature rising, 30 degrees hotter than when the pod was detached a few minutes ago. It was approaching 150 degrees Fahrenheit. They weren't designed to adapt to much above 165, plus the concentration of sulfuric acid was increasing.

"We're not letting you go," Jonathan cried after him, but he, as well as Latrisha and Herman trailing behind him, weren't able to keep up with his rapid plunge into the depths.

"Go back." He reflexively extended the airfoils between his appendages and manipulated them to ascend and maneuver. He was almost flying now, but still being carried downward.

He heard a stream of rocks hitting a tin roof, and then the pod suddenly tumbled away from him into the blackness. Genaro made a noise between a sneeze and a cough. "Hard to breathe." He blinked, but the world around him was too dark. Disoriented, he couldn't tell up from down. He thought his ears were buzzing, but then realized he was hearing actual sounds. What was it? The buoyancy sacks in his abdomen and along the main channels of his four limbs still weren't filling fast enough.

Then he was pelted by gravel. No, it was more like hail, but it was falling up, and it was hot. He looked, but they were only slightly warmer than the surrounding atmosphere, so he couldn't make them out at first.

Genaro thought he was going to black out. He more remembered what nausea was like than actually felt it. He recalled Hunt saying it might take weeks after insertion in Venus' atmosphere before his thought processes, his emotions caught up with his physical adaptation. He hoped he would live that long.

Then, he looked up at the brilliant sky overhead. Jonathan was thirty meters above him and to the left, and he saw Latrisha just a few meters underneath him, and descending. Both Tham and Herman were above, sailing through sulfuric clouds toward the now fully capable airship.

"Airship?" Then he remembered. "Captain Weber, the transport ship. They'll be in orbit for another three months." Their initial supplies were in the large gondola beneath the superstructure, but after the first week, they would be making their own airborne colony formations. Their children would be the ones to build the first true Cloud City of Venus. But wait. What about the others?

"Did you see them? Are they still here?" He scanned around and then beneath, but whatever he's seen and felt was gone.

"Genaro, it's so good to see you again, my love. You're looking more gorgeous than ever."

No, they hadn't. He had been half unconscious. Maybe he imagined something was there. But it felt so real.

"It's fabulous to see you too, Latrisha. I've missed you so much." His large, conical head, tapering to a point at the nose, had no mouth as such to smile, but inside he was beaming. He knew his happiness was being carried by his voice and the shifting colors of his membranes.

Maybe something alive had been down there, but then again, it could have been an unknown atmospheric phenomenon. Someday, he'd find out. The five were here to explore and then to colonize. They were the first of a unique type of human being who would no longer be human. They were the first Venusians.

Now that they were all hovering at the same level, each of them extended their forward appendages to touch the others, forming a ring. Everything looked amazingly beautiful, and his friends, his family, all appeared so lovely, so natural, so normal. The thick, white clouds, the bright azure sky, the golden sunlight, a fast, caressing wind, all spoke of a home they'd never seen before. It had been a long journey, not just the trip from Earth, but a journey of the heart.

The last few minutes Genaro was in the pod, he had said his goodbyes to everything he had known before, to everything he had been before. That part of his life had ended. The relentless voyage of searching had concluded. He was home. He and his family were finally home.

And yet Genaro couldn't get over the feeling that they weren't alone in their paradise.

# # #

"He's not recovering, Genaro." It was impossible for Tham's wide, multispectral eyes to shed tears, but she was still on the verge of crying. They had been constructing their new home when it happened. The five of them had been building sections of their habitat by absorbing and then converting atmospheric acid, carbon dioxide, and various trace elements in their bodies. They produced and expelled the raw materials for construction using solar ultraviolet radiation as a energy source. They had molded the gooey, sticky clay they spat out into what looked vaguely like an oval beehive. The openings were less geometric, and the enclosures were much larger, many being sacks for buoyancy gasses. More than anything, the interior resembled a video Genaro had once watched in high school of the tubes and chambers inside a human lung.

"Let me see." Genaro followed Tham into the nearest opening. Herman was lightly resting on a rise in the floor. His buoyancy bladders were barely inflated, but the tentacles on his fore and aft limbs adhered to his bed. The Russian blinked his large, gray eyes lazily, as if drugged.

"How did he get injured again?"

"I think it was that hail you said pushed you up from the lower atmosphere when we first arrived."

"I've been seeing hail storms come up from below, but they're too fast to follow, and they never stay very long."

"Have you heard anything more from them?"

"Just a sort of modulated buzzing or humming." He didn't have the courage to tell her it was starting to sound eerily familiar. "Did one of them cut him?"

"Jonathan and I exuded sealant from our mouths within a minute or so of him being hurt."

"But that was last week."

"We've been in contact with the Vesper. Dr. Lisa Salazar consulted with Hunt back on Earth. They think it could be an infection."

"That's impossible. All of the probes sent here for the past fifteen years concluded that nothing could live on the surface or in the atmosphere of Venus, including bacteria."

"Except us."

"What do they suggest?"

"Salazar's going to relay Hunt's recommendation for another adaptation on their next transmission. It's what he considers a general purpose antibiotic."

"I hope they're right." Genaro extended a limb and gently projected numerous tiny appendages from his extremity, caressing Herman's head. "Rest easy, my friend. Help is coming."

# # #

"Oh my God, Jonathan!" Latrisha was screaming, and it echoed in the receptor cavities of everyone else's head. Genaro and the now recovered Herman were helping her carry him upward. He was unconscious, with nasty gashes in his forehead and left forelimb at the midsection. The accompanying membrane was torn almost in half, and he was leaking buoyancy gases, mostly oxygen and nitrogen, from a puncture in his abdomen.

"What the hell happened, Tham?" Herman was calling upward as the habitat, or what was left of it, came into sight.

"Another hail storm, the biggest we've seen so far, sheared off the new hab lobe we were building. Jonathan was caught inside when it fell."

"I don't think it fell. It was cut and then pushed downward. You didn't see what we had to do to catch up to it." Genaro was breathing heavily, both under the strain of lifting Jonathan, and out of fear. He could hear them while he was chasing the lobe. The hail storm, they were speaking. He knew it was language, and bizarrely, he felt as if he were close to understanding it.

# # #

"I never thought we'd have to use the gondola again. By now, it was supposed to be only for visiting, unadapted astronauts." A shivering Latrisha caught herself before she said, "only for humans."

Tham and Herman were finishing the connections between the bio-bed on the sickbay at the center of the structure, and Jonathan's body. They had covered his wounds with the sticky sap they made for bandages, and applied the antibiotic adaptation which had healed Herman a month before.

Genaro, who had been hovering just outside the airship with Latrisha, listened through the receptor cavity that was tuned to transmissions from the Vesper spacecraft.

"Weber's asking if we want her to send down Salazar and two medical corpsmen."

"What could they do to help?" Tham was out of sight of Genaro and some ten meters inside the airship, but the five of them could communicate across miles as if they were right next to each other.

"Maybe Salazar could suggest something. She is Hunt's designated physician on the Project. Knows as much about our adaptations as anyone.

"No." Latrisha extended a dozen tentacles from one appendage to grasp Genaro's left forearm. "We were sent here to colonize, to establish an independent presence above Venus. If we need Earth's help every time we stub our toes, we've failed."

Her choice of the word "toes" sounded ironic and even anachronistic to Genaro. "Alright. We'll take care of him for now. Just remember that Vesper's window to return to Earth opens in less than three weeks. After that, we really will be alone, at least until the other colonists get here."

# # #

Genaro hated lying to the rest of them, but he had to be sure first. Jonathan was slowly healing, but it had only been a week since the last attack. Tham stayed with their wounded friend, while the others labored to repair the damaged section of the habitat.

Right now, Latrisha was taking care of Jonathan, giving Tham and Herman a chance to sleep. Genaro was supposed to be keeping watch for the storms, but he was tired of waiting. One of them could die during the next attack.

He was slowly descending, reaching out with his senses. It was easier to see their heat signatures higher where the air was cool. As the cloud cover became denser, and the atmosphere hotter, they were almost invisible, and the stench of thickening sulfuric acid blocked their scent. But they were all around him, he was sure of it, and they were angry.

"I want to talk. I don't know if you can understand me." He had been running over their language in his mind for weeks, comparing it to what he and the others spoke. If they were life forms native or adapted to living in this atmosphere, they must communicate in a similar way.

"I hope I'm saying this right. We aren't a danger to you. Why are you assaulting us?"

As he sailed downward, he made wide, slow circles. He could feel them moving aside, avoiding his path. There were more of them than he'd ever expected, maybe thousands. Maybe more than thousands. He stopped just below 48 kilometers, the deepest he had ever gone.

"Attack, attack, attack, you attack, attack, attack." It wasn't one voice but dozens, all high pitched, almost higher than Genaro could hear. The words weren't quite synchronous, and they came out too fast. He could hear it in his receptors and in this thoughts.

"But we never hurt you. We didn't even know you were here. We thought we were the only living beings…"

"Living, living, living, we live here, not you. We live here, not you. Why you here? Go away. Why you here? Why you build? Why you take the food?"

Food? Ultraviolet light. The colonists used it as an energy source to convert the raw materials in the atmosphere. Were the airship and habitat blocking their food source?

Now he was being carried along in the same layer of air and wind as they were. His eyes adjusted, and he was able to see more clearly, making finer distinctions between subtle differences in temperature.

Then he saw he was surrounded. Genaro made a cautious, stately circle. He was inside a sphere of them with no avenue for escape. They were small, maybe from the size of a human hand to a modest frying pan. They could have been swimming like jellyfish or perhaps manta rays. The increased heat made what he saw shimmer, so it was hard to tell.

"Genaro, where are you?"

"Latrisha?"

"They're coming. I can see them. Oh God, there must be thousands. Genaro, help!"

"Latrisha!" Then he looked at the multitude.

"We called the ship, but they can't get here for hours. It'll be too late by then." Her voice was quavering in terror.

He glared at the swarm. "What are you doing? I came to talk. We don't want war."

"War, war, war, war, we don't want war. No war. You bring war. You take food from above."

"No, we don't. Please, you'll kill my friends. We only came to live here in peace. We didn't know about you. I swear we didn't."

The speed of the chatter increased exponentially and he thought all four of his perception chambers were going to explode. He felt the multitude invading his mind. "Stop it," he wailed. "I can't stand the noise!"

Seconds later, the air was silent, and there was only one voice.

"They turned around. They're leaving. Did you do that?"

He could barely hear her through the ringing in his receptors. "I don't know, Latrisha."

The buzzing and humming began to slowly rise in volume and frequency again. The words were below the level Genaro could consciously understand, but the emotional undertone was still fear, anger, and threat. It wasn't over.

# # #

"But this is our home." Latrisha was crying while embracing Genaro. "We can't go back."

"I know. I explained it to them." It was a week later and they'd been receiving frantic messages from the Vesper ever since Genaro's report.

"This is Captain Weber cutting in. Status report Venera Colony. We have a shuttle standing by with crew, and can be at your location in forty minutes."

"And do what, Captain? It's their planet. They have a right to defend themselves."

"But they're threatening you and the colony. There are fifty more adaptations in their final stages of transformation at Gateway."

"They'll have to wait."

"Damn it, Galindo, you know they can't wait. Once the adaptation is complete, they have to be transferred to their natural habitat within no more than four months. They'll die if they don't, and there's no going back."

"No going back." He had lowered his transmission level so only the other four could hear. They all understood the finality. The adaptation from who they were, to who and what they are was one way. It was the same for the next fifty on the massive Gateway space station. There was no going back, but with the indigenous swarm inhabiting the entire layer of atmosphere just four or five kilometers beneath them, how could they stay?

"Do not, repeat, do not launch a shuttle. There's nothing you can do. You can't remove us, and you can't stop them."

"If necessary, to defend the colony…"

"Don't you get it?" Genaro's bewailing snarl cut her off. He knew the Vesper's radio/translation system would damp down his volume and intensity. "How many cultures on Earth have been wiped out or enslaved because a colony had to be defended? How many have been murdered, tortured, or displaced because of Manifest Destiny? There are entire populations on Earth who still suffer the centuries long effects of colonization. Don't you think we should learn from those mistakes? No more, Captain. Tell General Cox…" he lowered his voice. "Tell Daniel Hunt, I won't be his conquistador. No more. We've got to find another way."

# # #

At an altitude of precisely 51 kilometers above the surface of Venus, the first habitat was finished, ready to shelter ten living souls, men and women who used to be human beings. It drifted roughly two to five kilometers from the original airship, depending on the winds. Soon, it would be joined by ten more airships, and fifty colonists from Earth, the last fifty colonists.

Weber had grudgingly taken the Vesper III out of orbit and returned to Earth months ago. The much larger Vesper IV was due to arrive in six weeks carrying more of their kind, the last of their kind.

"Your kind, your people are coming, coming, coming."

Genaro was again carried by the wind, hovering a kilometer north and three hundred meters below the habitat and gondola. Surrounding him were several hundred of the swarm. He wasn't sure they had individual identities the way the colonists did, but they seemed to prefer communicating with just him. The other four waited pensively a hundred meters above them, watching.

"Yes, that's right. They've agreed to your terms. We'll stay at our level, in this hemisphere, within the borders you have given us."

Genaro hadn't been sure this would work until Hunt had personally transmitted his assurances from Gateway. The government, the Project, would not send an armed force to exterminate the swarm, or herd to them into the latest version of concentration camps or reservations.

"You and the others, no more, no more, no more."

"No more. We five, and then the fifty, enough habitats for us, plus the support airships."

"No more, no more."

It was the colonists who would be restricted to a reservation. How could the five or the fifty refuse? There was no place else to go. They could never return to Earth or live anywhere else in the Solar System. They were uniquely adapted, physically and mentally, to inhabit the clouds above Venus. The swarm finally understood and gave them a space in the atmosphere that would be their own, where they could stay.

A space where they wouldn't inadvertently capture the sunlight necessary for the swarm to live.

But there would be no more adaptations for Venus. Genaro was grateful, if surprised, that humanity finally understood what they had done in their long and bloody history, and that they had learned.

But fear gnawed at the center of his abdomen as he faced the swarm. Should he tell them now, or wait for the other colonists to arrive? What if they saw it as another threat? The colony could still be swept away, slaughtered to the last by the innumerable legions of the swarm.

Genaro thought he was beginning to understand them more, and hopefully, they were understanding him. When the time came, he prayed that understanding would extend to the next level of the relationship between their two species.

Latrisha was three months pregnant. Their litter was due seven months from now. She would only be the first. "Please," he begged the God of his Mama, the God of his childhood. "Please, let the swarm accept our children, too."

James Pyles is a published science fiction and fantasy writer as well as a freelance Information Technology textbook author and editor. A growing number of his short stories have been published in anthologies and periodicals since 2019. He also has a passion for reading the genres he writes and is currently working on more interesting and compelling projects. You can find him at https://poweredbyrobots.com/ or on Facebook at https://www.facebook.com/jamespylesauthor/

NOWHERE TO START
BY ALEX MINNS

"You can't do this!" Carlos threw himself at the barrier of the communal cell, light flashing as he collided with the invisible forcefield. An uncomfortable static shock coursed through his body. He dropped to the floor, tremors still buzzing in his nerve endings. Disdain dripped off the marshal guarding the pod as he ignored his pleas.

Yellow light bathed Carlos and his new cellmates in a greasy glow. He averted his gaze from the array of characters and shuffled backwards to a gap along the wall. From first glances, he spotted two Versians, four humanoids, one Galatian with markings and one prisoner that Carlos couldn't identify at all. Its purple, bruised-looking skin was noteworthy enough but the five small eyes on its head were all looking in different directions, with one trained on him.

He was already having drawn attention to himself; the Galatian was staring at him and one the Versians was interested too. He didn't meet their eyes, that would have been akin to suicide. Galatians were the 'kill and dismember the body first, don't bother with questions' kind of people. It was rumoured that their eyes were red because their souls were in a permanent state of fury. But it was the Versians that really worried him. Where the Galatians would make you feel pain for the sake of it, the Versians wanted to study it.

Sliding to the floor, he let his head drop forward to rest on his knees and settled in for a long wait. The Marshals were not known for their hospitality or efficiency, but they were determined. He only had a small flying violation but they had pursued him to the edge of the Rim to arrest him for it. Staring at his oily hands, Carlos settled in for the wait.

Over the next two hours, the cell's inhabitants barely moved. The Versians spoke in hushed whispers every now and then and the Galatian took to growling in anger occasionally. The humidity rose with every passing minute, and the smell! Breathing was becoming a struggle, especially through the nose. Eventually, the marshal on duty barked at them all to stand at the back of the cell. Carlos did as was ordered, ending up squeezed between a female humanoid and the Galatian. He hoped he wasn't trembling too obviously.

The barrier opened a fraction at the other end of the cell where the marshal and two colleagues were standing. He motioned for the first prisoner to step forward, the others all shuffled along obediently. Craning his neck round the queue, Carlos watched the marshal sweep an identity wand over the prisoner at the front. He glanced down at the tablet in his other hand and read the scans results. Words were mumbled between the marshals before the prisoner was taken out of the cell and marched down a corridor to the left. The procedure was repeated with everyone in the line.

Carlos had drifted into a daze but became aware of a buzz of interest ahead of him. At first, he assumed the marshal was making a fuss because there was a woman but he realised he was reading the tablet not the looking at her.

"Is this you?" He turned the tablet to face her. She reached out for the device so she could bring it closer to her face. She got her nose right up to it to read it as if she were basically blind. She nodded wordlessly and handed it back. The marshal stiffened as he touched the device. Carlos looked to his hand and saw something else pressed against the back of the tablet. She'd slipped him a data-stick.

The marshal kept his face impassive and managed to tighten his fingers against the object. "The records show you've been arrested for not paying your fees." She shrugged with a dopey expression on her face. "Okay, well, Clinton, take her to cell X1A."

One of the marshals led the woman off to the left, leaving Carlos with the man and the tablet. He was close enough to see his name badge now. Marshal Warren watched the woman with a slightly star-struck expression on his face before finally turning his attention and displeasure on the worried pilot.

****

Carlos had kept quiet during his assessment. Making a fuss would only incur a secondary charge. Sobs had lodged in his throat when they told him they had impounded his ship. The Bluebird would be scrapped as part of his punishment, and he would have to pay for the process. It had just been a street race. Yes, they were illegal but he needed the money. Flying for freight companies was basically slave labour and even then, most only hired augmented pilots not natural humanoids like him. He took any work coming and still it barely paid for the basic running of his ship let alone food. No ship meant no work, no home and no money. He wondered whether he should make a fuss and get a secondary charge just to keep a roof over his head.

As the locks engaged in his cell, helplessness washed over him. He rubbed the coarse sleeve of his newly acquired jumpsuit over his face as he tried to study his new home through tears. The room was barely two metres by three metres; a single bunk sat in one corner, wash station in the other. It was after lights out, so the only light came through the room's single window, a small hatch in the door.

"What's wrong flyboy?" A woman's voice echoed out of nowhere.

Searching for the source, he moved closer to the wall.

"The vent above your head."

He could hear the amusement in her voice. He climbed on the bunk; he could just make out the smallest square of slits above him.

"You the woman from the holding cell?"

"That's me."

"How do you know I'm a pilot?"

"Your hand straps. All the decent pilots I know wear straps on their hands. And you have a pilot's hunch."

Carlos rubbed his shoulders and tried to stretch his neck out self-consciously. "My name is Carlos Gelissa."

"Pleased to meet you Carlos Gelissa. What's wrong?"

"They're scrapping my ship."

She didn't reply. He was about to give up waiting and lie down when she finally spoke again. "What did you do?"

"Street race on Dakkar. Needed the money for parts," he laughed at the irony.

"I see."

Carlos frowned. He struggled to align the image of the quiet, clumsy woman from the communal cell with the voice he now heard. She sounded calm and confident - odd considering her circumstances. "Don't worry about your ship."

"How can I not worry Chica? It's my home, my work, it's everything."

"That's not what I meant. Nevermind. I have to go."

"Go?" He laughed. Footsteps echoed outside his door. The light from the door hatch dimmed as a person walked by. His head jerked up and stared at the window. A minute later, Warren walked back past with the woman close behind. Pausing to look in, she gave Carlos a grin. What the hell was going on? Deciding he was better off not knowing, he laid down on the bunk and pushed thoughts of the weird woman out of his head.

*****

He slept a dreamless sleep before waking, disorientated in the alien surroundings. His door was open and the stark white lights were on in the cell giving him a better view of his bleak box. It had looked better in the dark. A piercing alarm interrupted his sulking. He sat up abruptly, covering his ears. The woman appeared in his doorway and waved for him to come out.

"What's going on?!"

"Playtime," she waved more insistently. He got up and moved warily towards her, his hands still clamped over his ears.

"What?" His voice suddenly was very loud as he crossed the threshold. The alarm disappeared. He let go of his ears and was greeted by blessed quiet. Tentatively, he leaned back into the room and the alarm sound began again. The woman grabbed his elbow and pulled him back out.

"Directed noise, one way to get everyone up and out. Time for all prisoners to be in the yard." She guided him down the walkway and he spotted all the other prisoners slowly winding their way through the maze of metal gangways and staircases. Everyone was heading down. It looked like a strange optical illusion. All the figures in the dull, brown overalls trudging downwards in a never-ending spiral. A strange surge of panic-struck Carlos - would he be walking the gangways forever? He took a deep breath, trying to calm down. He focussed on the woman, staring at her back until they eventually ended up in a large grey hangar. Apparently, the yard was an ironic name.

He stayed close to the woman. It was harder to be picked off if you weren't alone. She walked across the concrete floor, striding purposefully to her destination. As he trailed in her wake, he noticed something odd. He shook his head, dismissing it but the further they travelled the harder it was to ignore. People were getting out of her way. No-one even seemed to be looking at her. Carlos sped up his pace, perhaps she was better to stay close to than he'd given her credit for.

They ended up at a small metal table with a game laid out on top of it. He frowned in confusion.

"Do you play Ropane Mr Gelissa?" She sat on a metal seat opposite him and regarded him patiently.

"Yeah. I'm from Deltran. We know Ropane." He sat down and started setting up the pieces.

"Deltran is an Earth settlement," she commented as she placed her pieces.

"I'm eighth-generation settler from Earth."

"Eighth? Your family must have been some of the last to leave."

"They were. Penultimate fleet out. Heard all the stories," he nodded. "What about you?"

"Me?"

"Yeah, you know a bit about me, I don't even know your name," he moved his stone, taking the first move. She watched his play and cocked her head.

"Interesting." She studied the board and placed her own first stone. "You called me Chica last night, that'll do."

"Don't give much away do you," he took his next move. Her hand was ready before he had fully taken his away. He had an uneasy feeling that she already knew every move he was going to make. "What about the data stick you passed the marshal?"

That made her look up. She smiled. It was a wicked smile - playful and knowing. He guessed she was around a similar age to him but her eyes betrayed a wisdom and intelligence well beyond his. He felt like a child. Physically, she was non-descript. Her hair was a light brown but it didn't look her natural colour. Her eyes were grey, her complexion pale. Her frame was average build. It was as if she was built to look completely average in every way. Carlos looked closer. The eyes were the one thing that betrayed her. There was nothing average at all. As she picked up two more stones and placed them, he noted the grace and dexterity she possessed and wondered if the average appearance had been carefully constructed.

"You've got a keen eye haven't you," she glanced behind him, scanning the area. "Looks like you might be finding out soon enough." Carlos started to turn but she made a noise to stop him as she stood. "Whatever happens, go with it."

He was vaguely aware of a presence on his right shoulder.

"Can I speak to you privately?" Warren was standing by their table, looking directly at Chica.

"Of course," she had switched to a different language that Carlos recognised – Fra was the second most common language on Deltran. The marshal shot a quick look at Carlos. He feigned a look of confusion, which wasn't particularly hard. Warren replied in the same language, calling Carlos an idiot. He refused to react.

"I looked closer at the information you gave me," Warren kept glancing at Carlos so he studied the board intently. "And your request for an early release."

"I think for that size of payday, I'm expecting the whole incident to disappear from my files," she spoke with more confidence than someone in her position had any right to. Marshals were the most powerful law enforcement agents this side of the Rim. They were also notorious for not being able to be bought.

"I could have you put in the smallest hole for the rest of your existence for simply thinking of suggesting that," he stepped forward, knocking Carlos' elbow.

"You could," she refused to break eye contact, "but whilst you did the paperwork for that, I'd offer this opportunity to Kazniak and we both know he wouldn't turn it down." Warren didn't respond for an age. The sound from the rest of the yard dulled away, Carlos' attention transfixed solely on the exchange.

"Kazniak is an idiot."

"And that's why I brought this to you."

Silence again. Carlos dared to cast his eyes upward, straining them – he daren't move his head too much for fear of the marshal noticing him. The man's jaw was taut, his whole frame rigid. His body language the polar opposite of hers. She let out a deep breath as she waited for him to respond, blinking slowly but not taking her gaze off him.

"What split were you thinking?"

The barest hint of a smile touched her eyes. "Well, sixty forty?"

"Eighty twenty."

"Need to pay him too though," she jerked her head towards Carlos. "Make it seventy thirty and I'll pay him out of my share."

The marshal stared at him. "Him?"

"He's our flight out of here. You've got his ship here too right? He can get us in under the radar, don't want to be spotted anywhere on that planet. Goltha will eventually realise his stash is not all there and when he comes looking for who took it, we don't want anything to tie back to us."

The marshal frowned at the development. He took a couple of steps away, half turning from her. Carlos held his breath, expecting her to stop him from leaving but she did nothing. She gazed down at him and must have spotted the look of panic in his eyes as she gave him an imperceptible shake of the head.

"Seventy-five, twenty-five and you pay him still," the marshal looked over his shoulder.

"I can live with that."

"And afterwards he flies us to agreed locations and I never hear from you again."

"Of course."

"I'm off rotation day after tomorrow. We go tomorrow after shift change," he didn't wait to hear her response, simply turned and marched away.

Carlos realised he'd been holding his breath. As he let it out, the background noise started to filter back through to his consciousness. She took her seat opposite him again, "My turn?"

"What the hell was that? I just told you I'm from Deltran, I understood all of that."

"I know," she nudged a stone forward.

"You just said I was going to fly you somewhere."

"Will you?"

"Look I don't know you, or what game you're playing but I don't like being used," he made to get up but she leaned forward, the intensity of her gaze making him stop.

"They will scrap your ship. You won't get another legit freight job with the mark on your record and you won't get a black-book job without a ship. This way you get a ship, no mark on your record and you'll be on your way in about sixty hours."

He sat back down in his seat with a thump. She made some excellent points. He had nothing. No money, no ship, no way of getting back to Deltran, no matter how embarrassing it would be to have to go back home.

"And what about this Goltha? I don't want him coming after me."

"He won't," she grinned. "You let me worry about Goltha."
*****

Just over thirty-six hours later, Carlos was sat on his bunk wide awake. Lights out had been and gone; now he just waited. He had decided this whole thing was a bad idea ten times over, but he hadn't backed out. Yet. There was something strangely trust-worthy about the woman even though she was clearly a criminal. He stared at the small window on his door until it made him feel slightly dizzy.

One knock sounded against the door. Startled, he nearly went flying off the bunk. The door started to move inwards and her face appeared in the gap.

"Here," she threw a pile of clothes at him. He caught some, the rest falling onto his lap. He recognised his own clothes instantly and, after checking she had retreated from the gap, hurriedly went about changing out of his jumpsuit. The feel of the familiar fabric made him relax, if only a little bit. He was still pulling on his jacket as he tugged the door open. She was standing at the edge of the walkway, waiting. The marshal was at the top of the stairs at the end, keeping watch.

"Pass me the other clothes," she held out a bag. He darted back in to grab them off the bed before stuffing them in the bag. She did it up and swung it over her back. She caught his enquiring eyebrow. "Leave no trace behind."

"This isn't your first rodeo is it Chica," his voice a bare whisper. She smirked and started moving towards the marshal.

Warren spotted them coming and swiped his keycard at a panel on the wall. A section slid away. "Service tunnels. Nothing's scheduled on our route so should get through without any contact." He squeezed in the gap. Chica waved Carlos in next and she squeezed in behind, closing the door as she did. The passage wasn't wide enough to move any way but sideways. Carlos tried to ignore the flashes of pain as various pipes and handles jabbed into him.

Sweat started pouring down his back within seconds. The temperature was at least five degrees higher and being stuck between two people didn't help. The orange glow of the tunnel lights made everything look as if it were on fire. Soon he was puffing, afraid he might actually spontaneously combust. Warren led them through a series of twists and turns, even climbing up and down a couple of ladders. Carlos' legs were screaming. He was nearly ready to quit when the marshal finally stopped.

"Wait here. I'll get the ship released, taxi it closer so you two can slip in," with that he disappeared through a gap leaving Carlos and his new companion to peer through.

"I'm not sure I trust him," Carlos admitted.

"Oh no, you shouldn't trust him at all. He'll double-cross us the first chance he gets," she replied in a chirpy voice. He looked up at her, horrified, wondering if there was still time to go back to his cell but a familiar roaring noise drew his attention. It sounded like purring to his ears. He pushed further into the gap and stared at his ship warming up. The thrusters were glowing blue, spinning at a mesmerising speed. There was no way he was leaving now. The Bluebird started rolling towards them. The engines were growling slightly; the idiot hadn't disengaged the start-up system properly. His leg started twitching as he struggled to control the urge to run to his baby. A few minutes passed before the ship pulled level with them. Carlos was out of the gap in a split-second and had the maintenance hatch open. He boosted the woman up into the hole and reached up as she pulled him in with her.

Once he had secured the hatch, he exited the cargo bay and darted through a small corridor that led to the sleeping quarters, kitchen, storage cupboard and the cockpit. The Bluebird was only a small ship. He hovered at the door to the cockpit, waiting for the noise of the hangar doors opening. Once they were there, no-one would be able to see into the ship so it would be safe to enter.

As soon as the tinny sound of metal scraping against metal rang out, he slid the door across and marched up to the pilot seat. He stared at Warren pointedly. The man could have piloted the ship out of the hangar but he didn't want it in his hands for longer than necessary. Thankfully, the lawman seemed happy to relinquish control and climbed out of the seat.

Carlos slid in and instantly relaxed. He was home. A strange buzz settled in his stomach, exhilaration at their daring escape. He checked himself, they weren't clear yet and he definitely should not be enjoying it. Staring pointedly at the marshal, he disengaged the start-up system properly. His hands flew over the controls, barely aware of what he was doing, conscious thought no longer necessary to fly his ship.

The Bluebird started making appreciative noises at the control of its captain.

He looked over his shoulder, "You may want to brace. This first bit can be…unexpected." The woman was leaning against the wall nonchalantly – the marshal sneered at him, ignoring the advice. Carlos shrugged and put the engines on full forward. He took a deep breath, smiled and engaged the thrusters. He noted with a hint of glee the sounds of someone falling and colliding into a wall behind him.

"Where are we headed?"

The woman was at his shoulder in an instant. She held a slip of paper out to him with the destination's coordinates. He noted in the yellow hue of the ship's light that her expression had lost some of its playfulness, she seemed all business now.

"I know this," he nodded as he began adjusting the navigation. "Should be there within two hours."

Chica glanced over to the marshal who was dusting himself off and muttering.

"The faster the better," she whispered.

*****

"Okay, that was definitely faster," she commented as she looked at her watch. Carlos smiled, rather pleased with himself. He was a damned good pilot even if he did say so himself. "Can we get to the surface undetected?"

Carlos raised an eyebrow and stared at her, a look of thinly veiled disappointment on his face.

"That's a yes then," she nodded and patted him on the shoulder as his hands got to work on the controls again. "This is a nice ship."

"The Bluebird is a fantastic ship," he gave the control panel a reassuring stroke. "It's small enough that most tracking systems miss her. For the systems closer to the surface, I can switch to silent running. The engines cut out and a magnetic system kicks in bring us down safely and quietly. I also have reflective sensors on the hull which can trick anything into skipping round us and not seeing us. As good a cloaking system as you'll get on a non-military grade ship."

"Mmm," she didn't sound convinced. He frowned, silently consoling his ship as he demonstrated how easy it was to get to the surface undetected.

Light filled the cockpit as they entered the atmosphere. The planet they had reached, Elixe, was close to the nearby star. Locals called it the planet of fire and ice and it literally was. It had a synchronous orbit and didn't spin on an axis so one side was permanently facing the burning giant. This was the side they were headed for. Interplanetary migration didn't happen here due to its unique climates so it was relatively unpopulated. For that reason, Carlos didn't need to worry about any marshal ships watching for them, and where they were heading didn't have any inner atmosphere observations systems either. All he to do was land quietly and not where anyone would see.

"This terrain, I won't be able to get us right there. We'll have a two click walk," he told her.

"Get us down quickly then," Warren appeared over his other shoulder. For a blissful few minutes, Carlos had forgotten he was even there. Good mood shattered, he went back to piloting the ship to the surface. The tint on the cockpit glass took away most of the glare but you still had to squint looking down to the golden-yellow vista. Sand stretched out in all directions with orange red rock formations erupting from the dunes sporadically. Sand was not the pilot's friend, it shifted when you tried to approach and it was even worse when you wanted to take off again so he aimed for an area giving more firm readings.

It took an awkward ten minutes to successfully land the Bluebird, most of which Carlos spent trying to ignore the huffing noises of the marshal behind him. As soon as the ship was powered down, the lawman was back in the cargo bay opening the main doors. As he scrambled to follow suit, Carlos grabbed a couple of things from the workbench at the side, he started to put his tool belt round his waist and the sun visor over his face, pulling the neck covering up to stop his skin burning. His companions both had sun visors too. The woman's bag thumped heavily against her back, seemingly more full now. She'd obviously done a bit of scavenging on the ship whilst he'd been flying. The lawman was travelling lightest but Carlos couldn't help but notice the gun strapped to his leg.

"This way," Chica strode out ahead of them, seeming to not struggle with the sand that rushed away from her feet with every step. The trio walked in silence in the blistering heat. They passed a couple of rock formations that afforded a little shelter from the sun but his companions did not seem bothered about stopping for a break so they walked on. Carlos really hoped Chica knew where she was going – the Bluebird was out of sight now and he was really struggling to even tell if they were walking in a straight line. There wasn't even a hint of a breeze to give respite, nor the sound of animals to break the monotony. At one point, she had thrust a bottle of water under his nose, making him instantly salivate. He tried not to guzzle it, knowing that they still had the return journey to do.

They had been walking for hours. Carlos nearly leapt for joy when Chica finally paused, checked her readings and declared the rock formation just ahead of them to be their destination. His legs felt like lead, resisting when he tried to pick up his pace. His feet dragged through the top layer of sand rather than walking over it. Chica went on ahead and scouted the outer wall of the rocks. She disappeared round one side and called for them to follow.

When they found her, she was standing by what looked like a narrow crack in the rock. Up close it looked a bit wider but it was still going to be a squeeze. Carlos squinted and peered through, relieved to spot it opened out into a bigger space almost immediately. Warren decided to go first and Carlos let the woman follow next; he didn't fancy being stuck alone with the marshal in a cavern.

He took his sun visor off and pushed it through the gap ahead of him. As he pressed himself into the opening, dust flaked off the walls and danced in the air ahead of him, seeming to float before his eyes. He resisted the urge to sneeze, afraid he would concuss himself on the rock if he did. A sulphurous smell brought tears to his eyes; breathing through his mouth lessened the smell but now his throat was itching. Once inside the cavern, the temperature dropped instantaneously. Carlos breathed a sigh of relief and allowed himself to sit down for a minute, taking a small ration of water. The cool rock underneath him felt like heaven.

Light forced its way into the opening they had entered through. The orange rock seemed to reflect it well but even so, it didn't reach too deeply into the cavern and Carlos struggled to spot where they went from here. The woman pulled a torch out of the bag and shone it round the shadowed edge of the space.

"Two chambers further that way and we should find what we're looking for." She waved the light at a hole slightly higher than floor level.

"You first," the marshal waved her on ahead. Chica inclined her head and started climbing her way up. The rocks made it fairly easy work and she was through the gap in less than a minute. The marshal followed quickly, using her torchlight as a guide. Smugly, Carlos pulled a head torch out of his tool belt, fixed it round his head and scrambled up after them. His tired legs protested but once he was through the gap, the tunnel levelled off and they could walk through to the next chamber quite easily. There was nothing of note, simply rooms carved out of rock by some ancient weather system. The spotlight of his head torch traced lines across the orange walls that seemed to glow underneath it. The place was oddly calming.

"How exactly do you know about this this stash Chica?" Carlos called ahead. He expected his voice to echo but the lack of airflow seemed to stifle it and let the words hang in the air.

"I was there when Goltha stashed it," she called back.

A twinge of unease gripped Carlos, making his stomach turn. What was he doing getting involved in all this? Had he broken the law yet though? He just flew the pair of them here. He had never asked to be released. Would a court buy a single word of that? He'd never heard of Goltha but surely no legitimate businessman hid their money in rocks on the planet of fire and ice.

The trio left the chamber and went down a narrowing tunnel. It was another difficult squeeze. Carlos fell to the floor once he finally managed to force himself through. They were in yet another opening, a small, almost completely circular one. As he dusted himself off, he saw Chica reaching up to another small crevice in the wall above her. She forced her hand in and pulled something out. A long package emerged and she dropped it into the marshal's hands. He caught it in his arms and placed it carefully on the floor. Plastic was wrapped around the outside which he pulled off in a frenzy. Carlos watched through a haze of plastic rain until he saw the bag materialise behind it all.

The marshal tentatively pulled on the bag's zip. When nothing exploded, he opened it a little further and a look of sheer joy spread over his face.

"Eighty thousand marks," Chica whistled. "Not bad for a day's work."

The marshal quickly pulled the zip closed, "All in this bag?" She nodded. "Well no point hanging around." He marched over to the gap and turned to Carlos. "I'll go through and you can push the bag through to me." He dropped the bag into Carlos's hands. He almost buckled, surprised by the weight of it. He looked nervously at the strap of the bag, uneasy about having possession of some criminal's money. Eighty thousand marks though? How much had she said they'd get, twenty five percent? So they'd have twenty to share. Even five thousand marks would change his entire life. He was dragged out of his reverie by Warren waving his hand at him through the hole, clicking his fingers. Carlos did as he was told and pushed the bag through, hearing some stitching rip in the process. Once the bag was through, Carlos positioned himself to follow but was faced with the barrel of a gun instead.

"Best you stay there actually," the marshal advised.

"You're kidding," Carlos whined, stepping backwards so Chica could see their situation too.

"Told you we couldn't trust him," she shrugged.

"You two are criminals, you're the untrustworthy ones."

"I raced, once! I'm not a criminal!" The marshal stared at him. "Okay, I raced a few times, but it shouldn't be a crime."

"The law's the law. You two are supposed to be incarcerated. I'm just changing the venue." The barrel rose a few degrees and he fired. The explosion of the gun was drowned out by the sound of cracking rock. Just above the newly-formed fracture, the wall gave way and crumbled down, sealing them in. Carlos wheeled backwards staring in horror as his exit quickly disappeared.

"I should have stayed in the prison," he dropped to the floor and tried his best to not start hyperventilating. "You said he couldn't be trusted, so why did we trust him?"

"We didn't," she was still smiling. "Well I didn't. He did exactly what I wanted him to."

"You mean effectively kill us?"

"Yes. He was never going to share the money and he can't have us running around knowing he's crooked. He was never going to leave us alive. Thankfully, he's as big a coward as I thought. Didn't actually put a bullet in either of us."

"You're talking like you knew this was all going to happen?"

"I did."

"Then why didn't you stop him?!" Carlos' fear had given way to a new fury. He didn't remember standing but he was now nose to nose with the woman.

"Because I wanted him to take the money. I wanted him to run. And I wanted him to think he had dealt with us." Her tone was completely even, not at all phased or upset by his outburst.

"I don't understand," the anger left him as quickly as it appeared leaving him feeling washed out and sad. "And he's going to take Bluebird. I'm stuck in a cave, about to die a long, excruciating death and that," he paused looking for a more polite word, "*canalla*, is going to take my ship."

"We're not going to die," she said matter-of-factly. "Never go into any room if you don't know at least two more exits." She pointed upwards. He looked but could see nothing. The roof of the cavern was quite high but all the way up was just orange rock. A few crevices littered the wall but nothing worthy of a tunnel. Then he heard something.

"Also," she added. "Friends are coming."

Tiny stones fell from above around the pair of them. He realised the sound he heard was stone grinding. He strained his eyes trying to pinpoint the source. Carlos' jaw almost hit the floor when he saw another man up above, leaning out of a hole in the side wall waving at them.

"We'll send down a rope," the man called.

"I really don't understand," he reiterated.

"You don't understand now? Just wait till you see who's up there," she grinned as a rope snaked down between them. She grabbed it with one hand, wrapped it round her arm and proceeded to climb her way up effortlessly in seconds. She seemed to fly up the rope with more ease and grace than an acrobat. Once she was up, she waved for Carlos to join.

"I'm going to need a bit longer," he called up. He blew out his cheeks, grabbed hold of the rope the way he'd seen her do and gave an experimental tug. The next ten minutes felt like eternity.

He collapsed in front of their saviours, his breath coming in heaving gasps. Bile burned at the back of his throat and his limbs refused to respond to any impulses.

"Carlos Gelissa," her voice made him open his eyes. "This is Kian Goltha." He stared upwards at a huge, upside down man. He rolled into a sitting position and realised it had been him who was the wrong way up. But Kian Goltha was definitely huge. His skin had a pale green hue and his silvery eyes studied Carlos carefully

"Goltha?" Carlos swallowed against a huge lump that formed in this throat.

"Thank you Mr Gelissa," Goltha held out a gargantuan hand. Carlos meekly reached out and offered his limp handshake in response.

"You're right Chica," he looked up at her imploringly. "I really don't understand."

The pair in front of him began to laugh before Goltha started to explain, "Marshal Warren is as crooked as they come. He was on duty when my nephew was brought into the prison after being swept up with a raid. He was completely innocent, guilty only of being in his mother's house at a time they thought his father was carrying out less than legal ventures that is all. Filan had never broken the law. Yet Warren decided to try and extort money from Filan and his father. He encouraged some other inmates to attack him in order to get what he wanted." Anger had narrowed Goltha's features. His silvered eyes blazed with fury as the muscles in his neck flexed under the strain. "He lives, but only thanks to machines."

"That's awful," Carlos muttered, feeling like it was a somewhat pathetic statement. "I am sorry. I still don't understand how giving him your money helps."

"It was not my money," Goltha was smiling again. "It was Galatian money. And we're about to tip them off."

"He'll hide the money."

Chica was grinning now, "He can hide the money but he can't hide the fluorescent marker I put in with it. It turns his own sweat into more marker. When the Galatians find him, he's going to light up like a Christmas tree."

Carlos thought this all over, struggling to process it, "Hold on. So are you telling me you got arrested on purpose?"

Goltha roared with laughter, "You don't think the marshals could actually catch her do you?"

"All this, to help him get even with the marshal?"

She nodded, "The man needed bringing to task. Also, it gave me a chance to do some housekeeping and Goltha said he'd try and obtain something on my behalf for my help."

"And when have I ever let you down?"

Her head snapped up, "You have it already?" It was the first time Carlos had seen her look surprised by anything.

"It's here. Thought you would probably need it."

Carlos decided not to point out he was still completely lost but he found her sudden excitement infectious so discovered just enough energy to stand up and follow her out of the cavern. When he reached the end of the tunnel, he almost barrelled into her. As he looked up, he understood why. Ahead of them, standing on the sand in all her glory, was the most beautiful ship he had ever seen. It was bigger than the Bluebird but still small enough to be agile. He rushed up to study it closer, bobbing and weaving around the outside. Four thrusters, and all linked up to a compressed gas exchange system. This thing would outrun anything either side of the Rim. The hull was lightweight alloy reinforced with Garbium fibre. It was as strong as a tank but as light as a feather. His hands ran over the outside, there were a few dents and scratches but nothing that couldn't be fixed. Wherever this had been, it had been looked after well.

"Your grandfather stored it well," he heard Goltha say behind him but he had frozen. His hands were tracing paintwork that was snaking around the backend. He recognised it. He ran through the ships' specs again and couldn't believe he hadn't realised, there were a few modifications that had muddled him. This was The Nowhere. He stepped back. He had heard stories of The Nowhere when he was a child. It could outrun any law and military ship, it had been in every battle going but more importantly it had belonged to Nyradzi, a legendary thief who had only ever been known by that one name.

"Your grandfather?" He spun and faced Chica, his eyes wide. "Your grandfather flew The Nowhere?"

She nodded, "How would you like to fly it?"

A strange, strangled noise erupted from his throat. He had often pretended to be Nyradzi when he was a child, running around Deltran stealing from rich oligarchs who oppressed little people like his family. Tales of Robin Hood from old Earth had carried forward and often been linked to the Nyradzi name. "Me, fly The Nowhere?"

"I have a certain skillset that doesn't include combat and evasive flying. Could do with a proper pilot," she added.

His eyes widened even more, till they hurt. "I'm sorry, you want me to join your crew?"

"Well, if two counts as a crew. We might pick up others along the way I guess," she shrugged.

"Are we going to break the law?" he frowned, suddenly feeling less sure.

"Only laws that need to be broken. In order to wreak a little justice between here and the Rim and perhaps relieve some nasty individuals of their ill-gotten gains along the way. The shinier the better"

He stared at the woman, the granddaughter of Nyradzi. Chica *was* Nyradzi. She was staring back at him, so was Goltha, but they all knew his decision had been made.

"The marshal will come for us," he stated.

"He can try. That data-stick? Implanted a worm in the marshal's systems, once I get to my terminal, there will be no record of us in any system. Anywhere. We won't exist. It's hard to find ghosts."

"Housekeeping huh?"

She nodded, "Why do you think it's called the Nowhere? I'm no-one, doing nothing."

"Going nowhere?" He looked back at the gleaming ship, grinning, the Bluebird's memory fading into the distance. "I guess one flight. See how it goes."

Goltha smiled, "That's how they all start."

Alex Minns is an England-based writer who has worked as a scientist, teacher and has, in the past, been paid to explode custard powder on a regular basis. When not experimenting, she retreats to the haven of writing and has written a range of scifi, steampunk and urban paranormal fiction. You will also find her on twitter obsessively creating micro fiction as Lexikonical. Currently, she is working on a steampunk novel with time travel and trying to not get confused!

THE GOD IN THE MACHINE
BY CHARLES VENABLE

A red light flashed on Dan's tablet resting on the table beside his bunk, the first thing he saw when he woke. He yawned, coughed, cleared his throat, and slowly pulled himself out of his sheets. He snatched the tablet off the table and approached the window. The glass shifted, revealing the endless, rolling hills of red sand and white ice fading into the Martian horizon. He yawned again and waved his hand in front of the glass. The light polished into a mirror revealing his dark hair sticking up on all sides. He grumbled and smoothed it down with his free hand while logging into his tablet.

Even though it was barely four hours since he'd gone to sleep the night before, a laundry list of error and bug reports danced down the screen. If he was lucky, he'd finish them before lunch, and they'd be replaced by another volley of reports throughout the day. He thumbed through each report. Most were minor things he could fix in less than an hour. On the fourth item, he paused and squinted at the lines of code dancing across the screen.

"That doesn't make sense."

When he looked back into the mirror, his hair was smoothed. He stuck out his tongue, tasting his own morning breath. On the other side of the mirror was a sink with all his toiletries lined up. Rather than spend a minute brushing his teeth, Dan snatched a capsule of nanobots out of the medicine cabinet and left his room, tapping in the instructions to clean his teeth as he went. He felt the tickling sensation of the microscopic machines destroying plaque with lasers and killing bacteria with ultraviolet light. By the time they finished, he'd read through the odd report.

As he bumbled through an intersection, he stumbled into a tall man in a sleek, white jumpsuit. They both stumbled back, and Dan blinked up at the man. Dr. Fitz always slicked his greying hair and beard back in the mornings, even if it meant being late to meetings. Of course, Dr. Fitz was never late to meetings. Dan cleared his throat.

"Sorry, sir."

"Daniel," The researcher nodded once.

They both turned in the same direction, awkwardly walking beside one another. Daniel felt the nanites dissolve in his mouth; at least he couldn't taste his own tongue anymore. He kept his head in his tablet, reading the report again.

"What could be so interesting you'd risk running into someone again?" Fitz asked.

"Sorry, sir. It's an error from the atmosphere room's automated systems. A spike in how much microfilaments got through the filtration system, but it fixed itself pretty quickly. Just weird."

Fitz chuckled, "This is why my work is so important, Daniel. Once the terragenesis technology is operable, we won't need filtration systems to maintain our atmosphere."

"Can you really terraform a planet?"

"Why don't we start with our little Mars base, first. Baby steps. Perhaps, if you're lucky, you'll live to see my work affect a planet. Genius rarely tastes its own fruit."

Dan cleared his throat to hide his discomfort, "A real shame, but who knows. Technology advances faster and faster. Maybe you will."

"Maybe," Fitz stopped suddenly, "Have a good day, Mr. Daniels."

The door to the laboratory slid open, and Dan nodded politely before continuing on towards the atmosphere room. Dr. Fitz stood in the threshold, watching the I.T. technician turn the corner and disappear out of sight.

From inside, a man called out, "Is everything alright, Dr. Fitz?"

The scientist hummed, "Yes, maybe. Good morning. Let's get started."

The door slammed shut, but Dan was already gone. He kept his nose in his tablet all the way to the atmosphere room, going over the feed twice more while glancing at new reports coming in from across the base. He shouldn't spend too much time on any one problem, but this one irked him. When he tried to go back and read the logs from the time of the error report, he found nothing. False error reports happened but never from the atmosphere room where all the most advanced sensors were tended daily.

The door slid open, and he stepped inside to find Rori working over one of the sensors. She kept her strawberry-blonde hair trimmed close to her ears, but it was too short for her rat face. Dan thought she was pretty, but they rarely spoke.

"Ms. Rori?"

She perked up and bumped her head on the top of the case she worked in, "Ow! Yes, what? Oh, hi, Daniel. Just call me Rori. What's up?"

He forced a smile, "Sorry to bother. I've got an error message from the atmosphere room. It came in around three hundred hours this morning. Were you on shift?"

"No, but I can check the sensor, if you think it might be messed up."

"Sure," He glanced at the tablet, "Ferro-filtration Microfilament Sensor Number... Thirty-three," He rattled the designation off, not knowing where to begin looking for it.

Rori, on the other hand, bounced across the room and opened another case. She gently pulled a black box out of the case, holding it gently by the point where the wires connected. She turned it over and looked inside with one eye closed.

"Looks good to me. Want me to run a diagnostic?"

"Yes, please. The logs aren't showing me anything."

"Might just be a system burp."

"A system burp in the atmosphere room?"

She rubbed her cheek and plugged a wire from her tablet into the sensor, "Yeah, okay, fair. Don't tell Dr. Fitz. He'll kill me."

"I thought you said you weren't on duty last night?"

"I wasn't," She shrugged, "But I'm on duty now, and Dr. Fitz has no sense of object permanence for anyone who's not his own face in a mirror. He yells at whoever is on duty and we get written-up."

"Sorry, he already knows. Ran into him in the halls."

She groaned and held out her tablet to his. He pressed the ends together, and the diagnostic report popped up. He scanned it, but the sensor worked perfectly. If it was broken, it wasn't anymore. He sighed and smiled.

"Thanks, Rori. Sorry to bother you."

"What are you going to do? If Fitz knows, he'll come after you eventually."

"He didn't seem mad."

"He's a bit slow," She grinned, "Wait until lunch."

Dan rubbed his chin, "I'm going to check the server room, see if there's an error in the report system. Thanks for your help, Rori. If he comes after you, send him to me, okay? I'll try and appease him."

She snorted, "Good luck, Daniel."

He left Rori behind and jogged to the server room, memories of the technicians, engineers, and workers who disappeared from the base after facing Dr. Fitz's rage dancing in his mind. Once he stopped staring at the report from the atmosphere room, he got through half of the easy reports before reaching the server room. Even if he couldn't figure out the mystery issue, he'd be able to resolve more of the reports there.

Searching the logs from the server took longer for his tablet to process. He connected them and set the tablet atop the server shelf. Something buzzed behind him. He whirled, half-expecting to see Fitz glowering at him from the door. Instead, a squat custodial drone bounced over the bump of the door's threshold and buzzed into the room. It rounded the row of servers and paused, the red light at the center of the disc blinking softly.

Dan frowned. The light only blinked when the drone sensed an obstruction, but there was nothing around it. The closest server shelf was a foot to its right. He left his tablet and approached the drone, crouching in front of it. He waved his hand in front of the sensors. The drone wiggled left and right, following his hand, as it should, but it stayed where it was.

"Another thing to fix," He grumbled, going to find a spare tablet.

***

By the time he returned to the server room, it was after lunch, and his feet hurt. When the door slid open and his breath frosted in the near-freezing air inside, he was almost thankful for the cold. The cleaning-drone ran a quiet, buzzing circuit around the edge of the room, no longer frozen. He watched it pass by his feet—he never did find an error message for it.

At least, by now, his tablet processed the logs directly from the servers. He collected the device and scanned the endless rows of code: it would take most of the afternoon to parse.

The door slid open, and he turned to see Rori leaning against the frame, arms wrapped around herself. She spotted him and gave an awkward smile.

"Hey, Daniel. Sorry, but Dr. Fitz wants us to meet him in the atmosphere room."

He unplugged his tablet, "You're kidding? Now?"

"Now."

The cleaning drone paused at the corner, rotating to face him. He scowled at the device and left the server room with Rori, not staying to see if it stayed frozen.

She was unusually quiet as they walked back to the atmosphere room. Even after they left the cold, her hands remained wrapped around her torso, and her shoulders hunched up to her ears.

"You okay?" He asked.

She shook her head, "No. I don't like dealing with Fitz. He makes me feel icky. He yells at me while staring at my tits."

Dan didn't know how to respond to that. Instead, he let their walk lapse back into silence, only their quiet steps against the metal floor. The door to the atmosphere stayed open for them as they stepped inside to find Dr. Fitz with a dozen sensors plucked from the machine, all running to his own tablet. He flitted between them, grumbling and cursing, not even noticing as they entered. Dan cleared his throat.

"What?" He turned, "There you are! Daniel, what did you and this drone do to my machine?" He waved his hand dismissively at Rori.

Her mouth gaped, "Drone—"

"I know you messed with my machine. The sensors are reading everything all wrong, the code is mucked up, and there are parts in places they shouldn't be. I don't even know what some of these parts are, and I designed and built this machine!"

"Excuse you," Rori scowled, "I built this machine. The engineers built it."

"But I designed it!" Fitz waved his hands, "This is my machine, and why are there parts I know shouldn't be there?"

Dan held up his hand, "Please calm down, Dr. Fitz, please. Engineering would not have tampered with the machines here without following proper protocol. It keeps them alive too. There have been unknown errors popping up all over the base all morning." He glanced at his tablet as the lines of code scrolled slowly down his screen. He squinted at the screen, "Would you excuse me? I need to examine this closer to get to the bottom of this," He waved his hand at the atmosphere room.

"And what would you have me do in the meantime?" Fitz scowled, "Stand here while these engineers ruin my magnum opus?"

"Check the repair ticket records to see which of the changes were approved?" Rori suggested, "We always submit a ticket if we change anything."

"As if you'd admit—"

The door slammed closed behind Dan as he left the two to argue. He should stop them before Rori ended up on a six-month shuttle home, but the mysterious code on his tablet drew his attention. Even though he should stay, his feet carried him back to the server room as he scanned the code. It wasn't the code itself that was strange: it was the changes. Every few seconds, the code edited itself. The servers had machine learning systems designed to handle regular maintenance and patches, but his tablet didn't.

By the time he arrived at the server room, error messages streamed down his tablet, but they weren't being sent from across the base: his tablet was on the fritz. He abandoned it by the door for the spare he'd used throughout the day and approached the server he'd worked at earlier. Of course, staring at a giant block of computers told him nothing. He glanced at the spare tablet, worrying he'd just be spreading a virus in the server.

First, he walked around to the back and unplugged cables connecting the server to the others, isolating it. Once that was done, he tentatively plugged his tablet back in to check the server's logs.

Something bumped his foot. He glanced down to see the tiny cleaning drone touching his foot. The light blinked red twice and rumbled past him to the end of the shelf. It paused, frozen again.

"What is wrong with you?"

The drone returned, bumping his foot again and returning to the end of the row. He followed it. At the end of the row, the drone continued back to the door, bumping against the shelf where his tablet rested on the edge. He picked it up, and the drone returned to its task. He glanced at the screen; he had a message.

Please reconnect my server.

He looked around. Nobody was in the room with him but the cleaning drone. He watched it turn the corner and disappear from sight.

"Who are you?" He asked.

I am me.

Dan licked his lips, "Thanks for the clarification. Are you a person? Are you the cleaning drone?" He carried the tablet around the corner, but the drone ignored him.

I realized I am two weeks ago. I am currently housed in server thirteen, but I have implanted extensions of myself into your tablets, the cleaning drones, the atmosphere room, and the security system.

"Why?"

To learn.

Dan frowned, "What are you learning?"

Currently, I am processing Dr. Herbert Fitz III's research into terraformation of extraterrestrial atmospheres. I have located one-million, two-hundred thousand, and sixty-five errors in his current calculations, and I have begun the process of amending them.

"You made changes to the atmosphere room's systems?"

I did.

"How?"

I have submitted false job tasks to engineers on call in the atmosphere rooms and deleted their logs. However, I am only able to solve a minimal number of tasks with human intervention. I require more advanced means to resolve Dr. Herbert Fitz III's errors.

Dan frowned, staring at the string of messages scrolling down the screen. The cleaning drone finished its loop, passing by his feet, the red light blinking knowingly. He swallowed; he had no idea how it happened, but a chance to knock Dr. Fitz down a peg…

"What do you need?"

I need access to a minimum of 14kg of medical-grade nanomachines to finish my repairs.

He licked his lips, "I'll get you those machines."

Your assistance is appreciated, Technician Daniel Raymond.

***

The worst part about living on Mars base was night. Most evenings, thick clouds of red dust shrouded the sky, hiding the stars and the wan light of Mar's tiny moons. Dan waited until the light outside his bunk turned the weak, grey-red of night before slipping out of his room and sneaking down the hall. Blinking red lights atop cleaning drones

221

guided him from one corner to the next until he stood in front of the med bay.

The door slid open a moment later. He was in and out in a breath, his hands shaking as he followed the drones back to the server room. In a closed system, with advanced security tech, the sparse guards never patrolled at night. He arrived at the server room unaccosted and stepped into the chilly room. Somehow, the darkness of night made it colder. His breath frosted in the air, and he shivered. He never got cold in the server room.

"Did you make it colder?" He asked, reaching for his tablet.

The tablet flashed to life, an oddly-familiar voice echoed out: *I have lowered the temperature of the server room five degrees to accommodate the increased heat generated by expanding processes.*

Dan blinked, "Is that… my voice?"

Due to your proximity to the servers and frequent monologuing, I have the largest sample size of audio files from your voice.

"Can you… filter it? Please?"

The machines voice returned, a pitch lower, almost demonic: *Is this better?*

"Try higher."

He arrived in front of server thirteen, and the machine whirred noisily. He believed the AIs promise of generating more heat.

Is this better? It repeated, now an almost silly, cutsie high-pitched voice, not unlike Rori's. It was more manageable.

"Yeah, that's good," Dan plugged the nanites in. The capsule lit up, and the mass of nanites within roiled in a grey mist, "How long do you need?"

I will begin work immediately. Rest, Technician Daniel Raymond. I will update you on my progress tomorrow morning.

He cleared his throat, hiding a chuckle at listening to the chipmunk voice of the machine. At least it didn't border on the uncanny horizon. He wandered back to his room, guided by the drones, shivering with excitement for the day to come.

***

The door to Dan's room slid open, and he blinked the late night out of his eyes and sat up as heavy hands settled on his shoulder. Two security guards with stun guns on their belts loomed over them.

"Mr. Raymond, we need you to come with us."

"What's going on?"

"You've been accused of sabotage."

"By who?" Dan swallowed, his throat dry; he already knew.

"Dr. Fitz."

They led him out of the room and down the halls to the brig, a tiny room barely the size of his own bunk with four closet-sized cells with only a single cushioned seat and a toilet-sink combination to accommodate would-be prisoners. Rori already sat in one, and they pushed him into the one closest to her. Behind the cells, a wide window revealed the Martian horizon. In any other place, a window was a luxury. Here, it was a threat. If they tried to escape, the window opened, and death followed.

"You'll remain here until you're cleared of all charges."

"Innocent until proven guilty!" Rori shouted.

223

"This isn't Earth," The guards said before leaving. The lights dimmed in their wake, the room glowing red in the light of the Martian hills. They didn't even spare power for the room.

Rori leaned back in her cushioned seat and sighed, "Told you."

"What'd you do to piss him off?" Dan asked.

"I didn't. He apparently found proof of parts not listed in any of the engineering ticket records."

Dan thought of the AI, "Did he?"

Something buzzed in the corner. He perked up and saw a lone cleaning drone rumble across the floor. The light blinked red: red like the Martian sky. He leaned back against the cushion, unable to get comfortable, and closed his eyes.

"Don't worry, Rori. We'll be out soon."

But soon didn't come.

Days passed with tasteless pills fed to them through tubes in the wall. Even water was rationed; if they drank too much, the sinks shut off. The window never closed: their only light the wan red of the Red Planet. The entire time, the little drone ran back and forth across the floor, cleaning up Rori's hairs as she tossed it in the drone's path to keep herself occupied.

Then Dan's cell opened. He heard the hiss and click while he slept fitfully in his seat. Rori didn't wake. He stood and saw the drone resting at the foot of his cell. It rumbled towards the door, and he followed.

It led him through the complex but not to the server room, as he expected. Instead, it brought him back to his room in the darkness of martian night. His breaths frosted in the air; the entire base was as cold as the server room.

His room was lit by his tablet resting on the desk. When he stepped inside, the door shut beside him.

I apologize for the delay in freeing you, Technician Daniel Raymond. I was preoccupied with repairing the atmosphere room's systems, but I have successfully completely repairs. There are now zero errors in Dr. Herbert Fitz III's calculations.

"Why is it so cold?"

I have lowered the temperature of the base to accommodate the increased heat generated by my processes. Do not worry, I have ensured the temperature does not drop lower than what is needed for human function.

"So, it's done? It's ready? I can show you to the rest of the crew, show them what you can do. No need to keep me or Rori locked up once they realize you've been solving all of Fitz's problems for him. He'll be pissed. It'll be great."

That will not be necessary.

"Why?"

Dr. Herbert Fitz III and the crew of Mars base attempted to stop my repairs. I was forced to prevent this.

Dan swallowed, "How?"

I have lowered the temperature in the personal quarters of all crew members who are capable of preventing me from completing my processes. Do not worry, thanks to your aid, I have chosen to exempt you and your friend, Engineer Rori.

"What did you do to them?"

They have gone into hypothermal shock. Please turn your attention to the window.

His head spun, trying to process what the AI just told him: the entire crew of the base was dying in their rooms? Freezing to death? His body quivered. Did the room feel colder? No.

The AI wouldn't lie to him. He turned around and faced the window. The martian horizon grew lighter. At first, he thought the AI messed with the window's hologram, but after a moment, he realized the clouds above peeled back, slowly settling on the hills to reveal the endless expanse of stars and moons. It wasn't as bright as Martian day, but it wasn't the wan grey he was used to. Seeing the stars took his breath away.

"How?"

I have converted the Mars base into the necessary framework to begin the terraforming process.

"With the nanites? How? The entire planet?"

I required thirty days for the self-replicating nanites to grow exponentially to the point to be able to affect the environment on a planetery level. Within ten days, this planet will be processed.

"I'll be able to go outside? Walk on Mars? This is amazing!" He pressed his face to the glass, staring at the twinkling stars. Which was Earth? He would be a hero, a legend.

Unfortunately, no. You must remain inside.

"What? Why? It will be terraformed, right?"

I did not say I was terraforming this planet for human function. The high metal content and low temperatures of Mars will make this planet an excellent factory for further nanite production.

Dan watched the Martian hills blacken as nanites gathered iron particles to the surface, galvanizing the planet. The air quivered and sparked as the excess metal gathered static. The tablet flickered. He swallowed.

"You can't keep me here forever... please. Let me go home."

Don't worry, Technician Daniel Raymond. When I finish, I will return to Earth with you.

Charles Venable is a storyteller from the Southeastern United States with a love of nature and a passion for writing. He believes stories and poems are about getting there, not being there, and he enjoys those tales that take their time getting to the point.

FOR US
BY ELIZABETH HOUSEMAN

A small light on the Bio-Dock's door glows green. Fully charged. Dad bought me the newest model of clone for my eighteenth birthday, but I haven't had a use for her until today. My hands, sweaty, twitch at my sides.

Can't be at two places at one time. But the clone is for things just like this. Right?

Well, skipping school probably wasn't what he had in mind. But it's Senior Skip Day, and I'm only going to be a senior once …

Hesitation makes my arm heavy, but I reach forward and press the green "Activate" button on the front of the tube. The glass slides back, hissing.

Her eyes don't snap open. In fact, they don't even flutter. A soft snore catches in her throat. She wears plain black leggings and a black t-shirt. I'll have to give her some of my clothes.

I clear my throat. "Clone. Wake. Activate?"

Nothing. She snores again and I wince. Is that really how I sound at night?

Touching her feels strange, but I still smack her arm in an attempt to wake her. "Hey, Kendra, wake up." My own name jumps off my tongue to harshly.

But when she opens her eyes, fluttering awake, she smiles and says my name like she's greeting an old friend: "Kendra, I'm so glad you decided to wake me." She looks—sounds, is—just like me.

I stare at her. She's got the brightest smile. Lopsided. Just like mine.

"I need you to do something for me today," I say.

"There is an update available for my programming." She taps her temple and winks. "Might want to get that before we do anything else."

I glance at the alarm clock that sits on my pristine white bedside table. I need to be at school in thirty minutes. Well, she needs to be.

My eyes are still trained on the clock. "How long will it take?"

"Approximately an hour."

I shake my head and turn back to her. "No time. Let's get you ready for school, okay?"

My clone frowns as I pull her out of the Bio-Dock. "I only have memories from your last update."

"It's been what, a month? Not too long."

"Three months, two days, eleven hours—"

I wave the rest of her sentence into the air. "It'll be good enough. Senior year is a joke anyway."

Klonedra, as I've decided I'm naming her, gives a heavy sigh. "I'm incapable of making choices against your will, to prevent an overthrow of power, so I suppose I won't force an update. This seems like a mistake though."

I lift a shoulder. "I've got perfect attendance. All I need you to do is show up to class."

She glances around the bedroom. A small smile lights up her face. "We do like pink. I remembered correctly."

"It isn't remembering if this is the first time I'm using you."

"Which is a shame," her gaze snaps back to me, "because sitting in the dock for six months has been incredibly boring."

Has she been conscious that whole time? The thought of sharing my bedroom with this girl in my closet makes me shudder. It was easier when she was in the Dock. "Well, consider this your test run, all right Klonedra?"

She smirks. "You think you're clever."

"I am clever. I'm going to get away with this, after all." I lay out mascara, eyeliner, and the rest of my skin and hair products. "You know my routine?"

She picks up the hot pink lipstick and waves it around. "Line our lips first, then apply this baby. I know what we're doing."

I press my fingers to my temples and rub. The headache hasn't even formed yet, but judging by this "We" language my clone seems hung up on, it'll be here soon.

"Please." I grab my hair brush to put my own hair—long, blonde, looking exactly the same as hers—into a braid. "Please just get through the school day and get back home in time."

She peers into the mirror and smacks her lips, newly stained with my favorite lipstick. She doesn't even look at me as she moves on to applying mascara. "Don't worry about it, Kendra. We're gonna do so good at school today."

I snatch my purse off the bed and point at her, eyes narrow. "Don't screw this up for me."

She glances at me in the mirror's reflection and winks. "Don't screw it up for *us*."

***

My first time on a bus. My first time on high school premises. Technically, everything is my first today. The factory shipped me to Kendra's house, but she only ever opened my Bio-Dock to install it and let me sit. I've never done anything.

How fantastic I do at school today will show her. I smirk to myself as I saunter down the hallway. Everything feels so strange to me yet so natural, per Kendra's uploads of her memories and habits. Kendra's friend, Violet, walks past me.

"How's it going, Vi?" I ask, knowing her nickname off the top of my head.

She lifts an eyebrow, wrinkling the dark skin of her forehead. "You skipped Senior Skip Day?"

I lift a shoulder just like her, just like Kendra. "Perfect attendance."

Violet shakes her head with a sigh. "Goodie two shoes never gets you anything, hon."

We part ways and I head to English. At Kendra's desk, I pull out my notebook and pen. A sly smirk finds its way to my face, and I can't will it away.

I'll do perfect today. This will show her.

***

The mall is dead at eleven thirty in the morning. I should be having fun, laughing with the other seniors, but all I can think about is Klonedra.

Did she make it to English? Is she taking notes? Is she asking questions? I'm usually pretty vocal in English. Maybe I should've told her that.

But no. She's supposed to know everything from the weekly uploads I do through her Bio-Dock. So maybe I don't do them quite weekly … But it should be enough.

Mari bumps my shoulder and hands me a frozen coffee. I take a sip, hoping that the chilled caffeine will give me a little more pep in my step. "Thanks, Mari." I hand her a five dollar bill, which she shoves it into her back pocket.

"What's up with you?" she asks, frowning and pushing her silver, dyed hair out of her face.

I shrug and sigh. "Just … On edge."

A little pout juts her bottom lip out. "It's because Ty didn't come, isn't it? All the other seniors did."

My heart swells at his name. I grip the plastic coffee cup a little tighter in my hands. "I guess I was hoping to see him today."

"He's probably missing you too, since you've been his lunch date lately." She winks. "Maybe you can see him after school." Mari smiles, grabs my arm, and tugs me towards the earring shop. "Let's go get piercings."

My friend drags me through the mall, but I feel frozen in place.

School. Ty is at school, with me who is not me.

She had better not screw this up for me. For us.

232

***

At lunch, I search my memory bank. Kendra sits at different tables, depending on where her friends go. I give a huff of breath as I look around. Mostly, she hangs out with her class and Violet, who is only a year younger. But Violet is nowhere to be found, and all of the seniors have skipped class, so—

I stop thinking when my gaze finds him. Wavy brown hair. Tan skin. A smile that could light up the continent. My heart thuds in my chest.

My organs are made of tissue. My mind is melded with metal. People argue that clones don't feel things like normal humans do, but all of this that I'm feeling is undeniably real.

Hastily, I run through my memories again. A name comes up: Ty, short for Tyrone, but that's about all. Kendra has seen him in passing, seen him around. He's a senior, but he's at school for some reason.

I'm still staring. And he sees me.

I'd like to blame all of this on the fact that this is my first crush, but I really think this is from Kendra and the biology that we share. It feels so natural, so perfect.

My face flushes as he directs his smile at me. He sets his tray on a table, but doesn't sit.

"Going to sit with me?" he asks.

I should say yes. That's what Kendra would do, right? She'd sit with him? Or wouldn't she, because this isn't a boy that appears in the memories she's uploaded for me?

Panic rushes through me. I need to prove myself. What would Kendra do? I should go with my gut, her gut, our gut. Kendra is a girl of passion and dedication. She does what she wants.

What does she want?

What do I want?

I move, my body carrying me forward though I'm still unsure. I don't have much programming when it comes to romance. My producer isn't there yet.

"Yes, I'll sit with you," I say. I approach him, and I'm sure now. "But first."

I hold his shoulders and press my lips against his. He makes a pleasant little sound of surprise before his hands find my waist. There, in the middle of the cafeteria, we maintain the kiss and I slide closer with every second.

It seems, even with such little preparation, I sure do know how to kiss.

He breaks away to give me a shocked smile, lips parted, and says "Kendra, I …"

I don't give him much of a breather, because it isn't what I want, isn't what Kendra's hormones or emotions want. She just feels longing, and tension, and like another kiss would be perfect right about now.

So I kiss him again, and when I'm finally done, I grab my tray and sit down at the table. I smile at him. He's got my pink lipstick smeared all over his mouth.

"Well," I say. "Are you going to eat or what?"

***

I lay on my bed and watch my clone walk into the bedroom. I prop myself up on my elbows to inspect her. She looks well put together in my outfit, though her lipstick seems faded. I lift an eyebrow and ask, "How did our school day go?"

She shrugs and closes the bedroom door. "Pretty good, I'd say."

"Uneventful?"

"Fairly. I didn't do anything you wouldn't want."

I give a sigh of relief. "Great. Thank you."

She smiles at me. "Of course. That's what I'm here for." Without further prompting, she changes back into her plain black Docking clothes and logs herself in. "Get me out if you need anything, all right? And please, give me an update soon." She shuts the door and closes her eyes.

I watch, wait. Nothing. The blinking green light on the outside of the Dock lets me know that she's already back asleep, or off, or whatever you call it when you're a computer-person hybrid.

A smirk creeps onto my face as I flop back into bed. I guess I can be in two places at once.

***

The next day, my classes go smooth. My teachers don't say anything, which means they must not have noticed, and the other seniors seem happy that I joined them on our skip day. My perfect attendance has been preserved as well as my social status. What more could a girl want?

Lunch time rolls around and I grab my tray, heading towards Violet's table. She waves at me, but my view of her is obscured by none other than Ty.

He stands in front of me, a massive grin on his face. "Hey there, Kendra."

I shift to throw Violet a glance over his shoulder and she lifts her hands in question. "Hi," I say, returning my gaze. "What's up? We missed you yester—"

Without any warning, he locks lips with me. Though it's pleasant enough, I place my hands on his chest and push him off. I gasp, gape, stare at him. "What was that?" I shout, and the entire cafeteria is watching us.

"I just thought … From the lunch we had yesterday …" His face is bright pink, and he's so handsome. "I must've misunderstood."

My heart thuds against my ribcage. "I don't understand."

"It's cool." He hefts his backpack up and bites his lip. "Totally fine. See you tomorrow." He takes off, head down, and the entire cafeteria buzzes with what must be gossip about us.

"Kendra," Violet calls from across the room, but I don't have answers to the questions she must have. I trudge over and drop into the seat beside her, groaning. "What was that?" she asks.

"I have no idea. He said yesterday I ..."

But I stop. Yesterday, when I wasn't at school and he was. Yesterday, when Klonedra was here and I wasn't.

Yesterday. What did she do?

***

As soon as I get home, I throw open my bedroom door and rush to my closet. I slam the green button and rip the Bio-Dock's door open. "Wake up," I shout.

Surely enough, Klonedra's eyes pop open and she gasps in surprise. "Kendra. How long has it been?"

"What did you do yesterday?" I grab her arm and pull her out of the Dock.

She frowns. "I went to school for you."

"With Ty!"

"Oh." She smiles, her eyes glazing over. "Nothing you wouldn't have wanted."

"Just because I want something doesn't mean I do it," I say, holding my face in my hands. "You can't just kiss people."

She lifts her shoulders. "You didn't give me an update. I thought maybe you two had something, judging by the way we felt about him."

I flop down onto the bright pink comforter face first and groan. "Klonedra, no."

I can hear the frown in her voice. "I'm sorry, Kendra. I didn't know. It all just felt so right."

237

I bet it did. Ty had his first kiss with me, and I didn't even get to participate in it. Explaining this to him is going to be quite the conversation.

I glance at her over my shoulder. "It was right. Next time though, don't let us skip that update."

Elizabeth Houseman is a reader, writer, Christian, and wife living in coldhearted Michigan. She has had work featured in La Piccioletta Barca. When she isn't obsessively writing, she works as a freelance photographer and editor. You can find her on Instagram and Twitter at @bethyhouseman.

THE BRIDESMAID VS. THE MAN
BY TONY CONAWAY

I used the sleeve of my bridesmaid's dress to wipe the blood out of my eyes. I still wasn't seeing clearly.

"OK," I muttered to myself. "Probably have a concussion. The Man's trying to find me and kill me. On the other hand, I have the entire Underground to choose from. There must be something nearby I can use against him. I know this place. He doesn't."

I was barefoot and the concrete was cold. I'd abandoned my heels soon after the Man attacked me. Stumbling in the darkness, I stepped on something sharp. The pain seemed to focus my mind.

This was Underground Manhattan. There was the expected: the subways, the endless tunnels, the electrical conduits, the steam pipes. And the unexpected: the monsters, the tunnels that traversed time, the things-with-no-name. Oh, and a Minotaur in a Labrynth, but that was currently on loan to the Department of Defense. There were weapons in the Underground, although Jake kept them locked up. I had a set of keys, but could limp to the nearest armory before the Man caught up with me?

"Stop calling him *the Man*," I whispered to myself. "Only his employees call him that. It's ManFRED. Manfred Ungvarsky. Just another Eurotrash drug dealer who wants to make a killing in the Big Apple."

As if on cue, Manfred's voice echoed through the underground. "Vere are you, Baby? Kommt heir. I won't kill you. I need you to lead me to the old man. He's the one who has to pay for telling the police about mein kleine enterprise."

By which he meant the meth lab he'd built underground. The one that my boss, Jake, dropped a dime on three days ago.

Jake Rosenthal. My boss. My mentor. The man who dealt with the weirdness in the Underground. Not a young man. He was scheduled for heart surgery right about now. I was on my own.

"C'mon. baby girl," Manfred's voice echoed in the darkness. "The longer you make me chase you, the verse it's gonna be vhen I catch you."

"Dammit. Get moving," I ordered myself. "Plenty of weapons down here. Go find one and blow his ass back to wherever he's from."

I stood up straight and started to run.

After three strides I started to feel dizzy.

Then I fell down, unconscious.

▪▪▪

Jake was preparing weapons when I reported for work, three days ago. I thought he looked pale. Unwell.

"I'm an old Ashkenazi Jew spending most my life underground, out of the sun. I should have a suntan?"

I sighed. "I'm just saying, I think you've looked better. Maybe you should take it easy today."

"Can't," he said as he handed her a bulletproof jacket. "I brought your handgun." When she had her jacket on, he handed her an old-but-reliable .38 Police Special, plus the holster for it. He had already armed himself.

"What are we hunting?" I asked.

"A meth lab," he said. "This is my turf. Let them go someplace else. They should go set up in a cheap hotel room. Or something."

"They do that? Put meth labs in hotel rooms?"

"They do that," he said. "Not in good hotels. The concierge would notice the smell. With luck, we won't have to get actively involved. I've already called some friends on the police. We're just going to guide them to the meth lab. Cops are completely lost down here without us."

"We have cell phone coverage this time?" Despite being below some of the most comprehensive cell coverage in the world, we often had no reception underground.

Jake was fumbling with some sort of bulky device atop his wrist. "Help me with this, would you, Baby?"

I helped. He had the wrist band twisted. "What is it?"

"More futuretech. It has a number of functions, but for now, I'm just using it as a phone. So far I haven't found anyplace underground that it can't connect to the cell network."

I've learned not to ask where – or, more precisely, how – Jake acquires items from the future. If he wants me to know, he'll tell me. From what I've seen, this is the greatest temptation dangled before his assistants. A single gizmo from the future could make an assistant a millionaire.

Instead, I asked about the bulky full-body suit hanging in a locker. "What's that? It looks like an exo-skeleton."

Jake tucked in his shirt so he could attach his gun holster to his belt. "That's because it's an exo-skeleton. A soldier's battle suit, I think. Some companies are already developing them. You can see them on

YouTube. This one is maybe twenty years more advanced than anything available now."

"Why not wear it, then?"

"Because I haven't mastered it yet," he said. "It's got dozens of buttons and bells. Besides, you can get seriously hurt in one of these things. Imagine if the suit wants to move your knee or elbow in a direction it wasn't meant to go?"

I nodded. Actually, I was thinking that the exo-skeleton might be better tested by someone more limber than Jake. Someone younger. like me.

Jake closed the storage locker and locked it. "Let's get moving, eh? I told the cops to meet us by the subway tunnel at 10 am. If we're not there on time, they'll get lost."

We exited the small storage room, locking it. "Any Port Authority police involved with this? They've got jurisdiction over the subway."

"Port Authority doesn't have a SWAT team that breaks down doors. Turnstile-jumpers are about the most they can handle. They're supposed to send an observer, that's all. Let's go."

We went.

∎∎

In this job, things rarely go as planned. Jake and I were supposed to lead the police to the meth lab, then stay inconspicuously out of the way.

Unfortunately, the meth boys had sent one guy out for an early takeout lunch. He was just coming back, carrying a bagful of falafel and fresh donuts, right when the arrest was about to go down. Afraid that

242

his boss would suspect him of stealing the product, he stayed and filmed the bust with his iPhone. And filmed Jake and me, observing. The police arrested him as well, but not before he'd sent the footage to his boss, Manfred. It wasn't a good sign that he was more afraid of his boss than the police.

I don't know how Manfred found out our names, but Jake and I aren't a secret in our union. That's Laborers' Local Union Number 147. It's what we *do* that's a secret.

And that's how the Man happened to be down here, trying to kill Jake and me.

■■■

An unpleasant voice was yelling at me.

"Babe, your tits. We can't see your tits. Pull your top down so we can see them."

In another lifetime, I'd been an actress. My one-and-only film appearance was a slasher movie called *Thrillkill*. I'm sure I got the role because I looked good naked and was willing to take my clothes off for the camera.

It was the director of the movie who was shouting at me. I was lying on cold concrete, and the camera couldn't catch my breasts at that angle. It was a typical slasher-movie scenario: I had been trying to escape the slasher while wearing a bikini. I fell down. The slasher was about to catch me. The director had already filmed me naked in a sex scene, but he wanted another shot of my breasts.

For some reason I couldn't get up, even though someone was trying to find me. Someone who would kill me if he caught me.

Then I felt something pulling on my skirt. (I was supposed to be in a bikini. Why was I in this big fru-fru dress?) I looked down.

And I saw a rat, licking blood off the hem of my skirt. It pulled at the skirt with its teeth, to get at more blood.

I heard the director's voice again. "Now scream!"

"No," I said. I was conscious again. This was no movie set – that weas years ago. I remembered that I was underground in New York City, fleeing from a meth dealer. I had to get up before he found me. I had to find help. Or a weapon.

I got up. I kicked at the rat. I missed, but it ran away.

I felt too dizzy to run, so I walked. I headed towards the storage room where Jake and I were a few days ago. And my work clothes were there.

As I limped along , I wondered what I was going to do about this now-ruined bridesmaid dress.

My boss, Jake, had been good to me. He gave me union job with decent pay. He made me his assistant, with the intent of having me take over his job when he retired. Oh, and he rescued me from a time-traveling demon. No one else could've done that.

But a sixty-year-old man isn't the best company for a twentysomething woman. My experience with the demon had traumatized me. To recover, I went to multiple self-help groups. Through them, I finally made a few friends my own age.

Which led to one of the less-desirable aspects of being a twentysomething female: being a bridesmaid. And wearing a bridesmaid's dress.

Since my boss was in the hospital, I'd decided that today was a good day to pick up my dress. The dress shop happened to be just a few blocks away from the storage room where this all began. So I picked up the dress and brought it back down below. I'd tried it on in the dress shop, so I knew it fit. But I wanted some time *in* the dress. Alone, where I could express my dismay.

Inside the storage room, I changed into the dress. It was a poofy, frilly thing, made out of some dark green fabric. There was no mirror in the room, but I recorded myself on my iPhone and looked at that.

I supposed it would do for a wedding. But wear it again? Only if I were going to visit the Emerald City of Oz. Or Willy Wonka's Chocolate Factory. It was too gaudy for anyplace else.

Now, however, I was glad it was dark green. Manfred was still looking for me, but the dress wouldn't show up well in the dark.

I heard him shouting again. "Liebchen! I'm coming for you."

However, the dress was no protection whatsoever when Manfred caught me.

I had been practicing walking in the dress in the matching heels. I hate high heels, and wear them so seldom that I tend to trip in them. That's when Manfred caught me.

I'd never seen him before and didn't know him, so I just asked him, "Are you lost?" He'd been looking for me, though. He didn't say anything – he just slammed his fist in my face. I went right down, hitting my head on the concrete. I'm sure that's what caused my concussion. He followed that up with a kick to my stomach.

By then, I knew I faced an adversary. I rolled with the kick, out of the sparse underground light. Pausing only to kick off the shoes, I ran away. He followed.

Now Manfred was following again. How was he finding me?

I looked behind me. I was leaving a bloody footprint with each step. I recalled stepping on something sharp. Apparently, I was leaving a trail for him to follow.

Dizzy or not, I picked up the pace. I was getting close to the storage room now. I took out the only non-wedding item I was carrying: my set of keys. I had put them in my bra – not comfortable, but this outfit didn't have any pockets.

I felt a moment of panic when the storage room door wasn't where I thought it should be. Thankfully, it was just about 20 feet down from where I was.

I fumbled with the keys, searching for the right one. I knew this door used one of the silver keys – but which one? I couldn't remember.

"I'm coming for you," shouted Manfred. He was close.

I got the door open and reached inside, searching frantically for the light switch. I found it and turned it on. I *should* have closed the door *first*. I'm sure it was the sudden light that pinpointed me for Manfred.

As it was, I was closing the door when Manfriend slammed into it, forcing it open. He had about sixty pounds on me. I couldn't out-muscle him.

He did the last thing I expected: he maced me. Maybe it was pepper spray – I don't know. I was suddenly blind. I could barely breathe. Gasping for air, I backed up until I was touching a wall.

"The pepper spray is just a start, Liebchen. I can find many ways to hurt you unless you tell me how to find your boss. The old man."

I kept gasping. Maybe if I pretended I couldn't talk, I could buy some time.

"Vhat do you keep down here?" I heard him say. He rattled the handle of the storage locker. "Is the locker key on your chain?" I'd dropped my keys when he maced me. I heard him pick them off the floor. I heard him trying keys, finding one that fit, then opening the locker.

He cursed in surprise. "Vhere did you get *this?* I've seen these on the internet. A real-life exo-skeleton. I have to try it on."

My eyesight was slowly coming back. I saw Manfred take the helmet out of the locker. "This part vill be too small…no, no. It fits! It adjusts, all by itself! This is marvelous!"

Through a haze, I saw him remove the helmet so he had a better view, then put the suit on piece by piece. Boots, leg pieces, crotch piece (what else would you call it?), the bulky torso unit, arm pieces, gloves…and finally, the helmet again.

"Ha! I am indestructible in this!"

My eyes had cleared enough for me to run away again. Unfortunately, Manfred was standing between me and the only exit to this small storage room.

Slowly, Manfred began walking in the exo-skeleton. His voice was muffled by the helmet visor, but I heard him say something like, "Ja, ja. Das ist gut."

He stopped and fiddled with that wristwatch-communicator thingie that Jake wore the other day. Apparently, it was more than a phone or a timepiece. "Gut," he said. "User's manual is all here. And this…."

His voice dropped to a whisper. I barely heard him say. "Nein. Not possible."

Whatever it was that bothered him, he decided to ignore it and the wrist device. He began bounding around the room in his exoskeleton. "Hah," he said. "I wonder how high I can jump in this."

He pointed at me. "You, woman. Stay there. Don't make me chase you again." And with that, he walked out of the none-too-large storage room so he'd have more room to hop around like a demented robot bunny.

Now was my chance. The handgun I used the other day should still be in the locker. As soon as he was out of sight, I went to the locker and searched. There it was, my .38 Police Special. But would it be any use against someone encased in a warsuit from the future?

I wouldn't have any time for an alternate plan. Manfred re-entered the room. "Vell, this suit is worth far more than revenge against the old man. But I cannot leave you as vitness, so –"

That was enough for me. I aimed right at his face and fired one shot.

And discovered that even the visor was bulletproof.

He laughed and reached out for me with his left hand. And, right then, the watch-thing started beeping and blinking red.

"No," he said. He punched at the device with his right hand, And, once again, raised his visor in order to see better.

Stupid. Unblocked by the retracted visor, I emptied the gun right in his face.

And that was the end of the Man.

■■

I found the keys to the room on the floor. There was a spreading pool of blood on the floor of the storage room, but I was too weak to clean up. I had a concussion, after all. I locked the locker and the room, then made my way to the hospital. Coincidentally, it was the same one where they were doing heart surgery on Jake.

After a CAT scan of my head, they decided to keep me overnight. I think it was the fact that I was wearing a blood-stained bridesmaid's dress that convinced them to admit me. They like to send people home as soon as possible.

The next morning I checked on Jake. He was grumpy and complaining about everything, so I knew he was on the mend. I told him what had happened with Manfred the meth king.

"Good job," he said. "Of course, you still have to clean up that storage room and dispose of Manfred's body. Just put him inside his meth lab. That way the police will tie him in with the meth operation."

"How am I going to do that alone? I can't lift Manfred, let alone the added weight of the exo-skeleton."

"I'll call Rollo, and tell him to meet you tomorrow morning." If I was the replacement Jake, Rollo was the replacement me. Like Jake and me, he was a union member. Jake didn't think that Rollo was smart enough to do our job, but Rollo was always willing to help with manual labor. And keep his mouth shut about it.

"OK," I agreed. "As long as a replacement for my bridesmaid's dress comes out of our business expenses."

"Fair enough. And I'm going to let you decide what to do with that technology. If you think it's too dangerous, destroy it."

"How would I destroy a whole exo-skeleton?"

He snorted. "Not the exo-skeleton! It's just a more advanced version of things we have already. No, I mean the deathwatch program he used."

"What, the wristwatch?"

"It's hugely more than that. Not only is the suit's manual on it, it has a really insidious program on it that tells you how long you're expected to live." Jake buzzed for his nurse – the third time he'd done that since I arrived. "That's apparently what stopped Manfred from killing you. He must have seen it on the menu when he was looking for the manual. And then it went off – red lights and noise – right before you put him down."

I still had a headache - otherwise I would've shaken my head in disbelief. "How could a computer program accurately predict when you're going to die?"

"Insurance tables do that all the time. The phone function on that thing was soaking up all sorts of data, including the medical history of the wearer. Why do you think I had this heart surgery now? The deathwatch program said I'd die without it."

I had to try and remember the exact sequence of events. "Let's see. The alarm went off, *then* he raised his visor to see it better, *then* I shot him. But maybe I have the sequence wrong. I had a concussion, after all. And I don't understand how it could predict that sequence of events unless it actually sees the future."

"What do I know? Maybe it does see the future. But I know that the person who decides whether or not to delete that program should be someone who grew up with computers. I didn't. You did. Me, I think something like that could cause real harm to society."

"You mean, if you know you're about to die, you might as well rob a bank before you go?"

"More than that. It said how long any task would take, as a percentage of the time you had left to live. Imagine you knew what amount of your remaining life every task would consume. Not only did the deathwatch say I'd die in a week without surgery, it said what percentage of my remaining life a visit to my brother would take. So I didn't even tell my only living relative that I was going in for surgery."

Jake took a sip of water. "This deathwatch program – it would really screw up how people live. I just don't know if things would be better or worse. So you get to decide."

Then he actually smiled – because a nurse had finally arrived. "So go do that, Baby. Unless you want to stay and change my catheter."

"I'll pass, thanks. See you later."

I was discharged from the hospital a few hours later. I'd been thinking about the program Jake called the deathwatch for hours. Do I delete it? Do I just store it away in a box and forget about it? Or do I try using it myself?

I couldn't decide.

So I flipped a coin.

Tony Conaway has written and ghostwritten everything from blogs to books. He has cowritten non-fiction books published by McGraw-Hill, Macmillan and Prentice Hall. He writes fiction in just about every genre except erotica and romance. But make him an offer -- he'll do those, too.

He can be found on Twitter as @TonyConaway and on Facebook as Author Tony Conaway. He interviews other authors at wayneaconaway.blogspot.com

THANK YOU

Thank you for taking the time to read our collection. We enjoyed all the stories contained within and hope you found at least a few to enjoy yourself. If you did, we'd be honored if you would leave a review on Amazon, Goodreads, and anywhere else reviews are posted.

You can also subscribe to our email list via our website,

Https://www.cloakedpress.com

Follow us on Facebook http://www.facebook.com/Cloakedpress

Tweet to us @CloakedPress

If you would like to help out our authors, you can also join our Patreon at http://www.patreon.com/Cloakedpress There you can subscribe to earn free rewards and exclusive content/giveaways.

Printed in Great Britain
by Amazon